FLAWED

THE BILLION HEIRS

BOOK 2

HELEN HARDT

VANESSA VALE

The bad boy brother. The by-the-books detective. A random meeting that'll change their lives.

Miles Bridger would rather be home in New York than stuck on a Montana ranch with his newfound half brothers, thanks to his deadbeat dad's will. Miles now works with bulls and hay bales instead of custom bikes. He keeps his sense of humor about the whole thing...until a dead body surfaces on the ranch and he and his brothers are thrown headfirst into a murder investigation.

Sadie Hopkins plays by the rules in her job as detective, so she's only too happy to turn a little naughty during a bachelorette party dare. Heat flares between Sadie and the gorgeous blond man she approaches, but when a high-profile case crosses her desk the next day, she's in for a surprise. The man from the bar is none other than Miles Bridger...and he's a murder suspect.

Despite this revelation, Miles and Sadie's chemistry sizzles. But the flawed Miles doesn't do relationships, and Sadie's past crashes into the present with a surprising discovery that could spell danger for both of them.

*M*ILES

"DECIDE TO COME UP FOR AIR?" I smile when Austin and Carly finally grace us with their presence at the dinner table.

Carly's cheeks are flushed pink, and Austin's hair is a tousled mass of brown. Yeah, they both look *just fucked*. Make that *just fucked on steroids*. They've been in Austin's room since he and Carly came back this morning.

"Actually, I was sleeping." Carly blushes further.

Right.

"You don't owe them any explanation." Austin gives her a pussy-whipped smile.

"As you know," she continues, "I didn't get any sleep last night because I was tending to your colt."

"Which we appreciate." Chance reaches for the platter in the middle of the table. The dishes are set out family style in brown clay serving platters. Salsa, chopped onion and cilantro, seasoned rice, and black beans. "I didn't see either of you come out for lunch so I assume you're starving. Louisa made chicken flautas."

"Who? Your cook?" Carly settles in with Chance on one side, Austin on the other.

I'm across from her.

"The housekeeper," Chance corrects. "She keeps this entire place running."

I introduced myself to the older woman when she placed my clean laundry on my bed. I'm not used to anyone taking care of me.

"Looks great." Austin takes the platter from Chance. "I love Mexican food."

"Yeah. Me too. The spicier the better." The robust scent of chiles has my mouth watering. I grab my cold Mexican beer, squeeze the lime wedge into the bottle, and take a long drink. Good stuff.

I'm about to take the platter from Austin when the doorbell rings.

The housekeeper—Louisa—comes in a minute later. She's in her late fifties with salt and pepper hair. She's in jeans and a green top, and a gentle smile tugs at her mouth. "It's Detective Peterson from the Bayfield sheriff's office. He wants to speak to all three of you."

Chance sets down his fork with a sigh. "In the middle of dinner?"

"Says it's important."

"I guess that's my cue." Austin rises and kisses Carly's cheek as Louisa leaves the room. "Be right back, sweetheart."

I have no choice but to follow my brothers out of the dining room and to the doorway, leaving my beer and grub behind. This isn't wholly unexpected. A dead body was just found on our property, after all. But it's dinnertime.

The detective is a few years older than we are. Solemn looking, with bloodshot gray eyes. He wears scuffed brown cowboy boots, dark denims, and a striped button down. He's armed with a handgun strapped at his waist. I don't recall seeing him as part of the crew dealing with retrieving the dead body.

"Hey, Mark," Chance says.

He knows everyone in town. In comparison to his relationship with the mayor, Chance seems neutral toward the guy.

"Chance." The man tips his head. "You two must be Austin and Miles."

Austin holds out his hand. "Austin Bridger."

"Detective Mark Peterson. I'm investigating the murder that took place on your land."

"Murder?" I cock my head and withdraw the hand Peterson hasn't yet shaken. "I didn't realize it was official."

"We're still waiting on the autopsy," Peterson says, "but we treat all dead bodies in situations like this as homicide until we can rule it out. That means the three of you—along with your deceased father—are prime suspects."

"Suspects? Now wait a damned minute." Austin closes the distance between himself and the detective. "Miles and I weren't even in the state when that guy met his maker."

"That has yet to be determined," Peterson replies.

I didn't see the body, but from what I heard from those who did, it had been in rough shape. He'd been there a while, stuck beneath the deep water of the creek until we broke up the dam and it receded.

"Doesn't matter," the detective continues. "As of right now, I'm ordering the three of you not to leave town until you hear otherwise. You need to be on hand for questioning. I hear you were in Seattle recently. Don't leave again."

Invisible insects bite at the back of my neck. Is this guy for real? "You've got a lot of nerve," I say. "We were the ones out there breaking up that dam. Would we have done that if we knew we were going to unearth a guy we murdered? If not for us, he'd still be out there."

"I've been doing this a long time." Peterson sucks at his teeth and tucks a thumb into his belt. "I wouldn't put anything past Jonathan Bridger's progeny. I admit, learning he has two additional sons makes my job a lot easier. All I have to do is drive to this ranch to find the criminals."

Yeah. He's making it pretty fucking clear where this is going. I'm no small-town boy. I'm from New York, and I can smell a dirty cop a mile away. At least one who likes to cut corners and not follow the evidence.

"You know shit about us," I mutter, my hands curling into fists.

Peterson shrugs. "Don't have to."

I see red. The guy's already pinned this mess on us. "You fucking son of a—"

I lunge, but Chance pulls me back.

"Easy, Miles," he says by my ear. "I don't know what you're used to in New York, but you can't manhandle cops around here."

Austin steps toward the detective, blocking me from him. "My brother's right. This is insane. You know Miles and I had nothing to with this. Our only crime is that we were sired by Jonathan Bridger. And Chance? The big lug wouldn't hurt a fly."

"You sure about that?"

A vein in Chance's temple throbs, but he says nothing.

"Why the fuck would he kill someone on his own land?" I ask.

Peterson shifts his gaze from Chance to me. "You have enough of it. Lots of places to hide a body."

I break free of Chance's grasp, but instead of flying at Peterson and rearranging his face, I stomp past him and out to the garage next to the main house where my classic Harley Softail waits for me. I bought it from the classifieds in the local paper the other day. It's in rough shape, but I know a good thing when I see it. Some TLC and she'll be incredible, just like all my other projects.

If I don't get the hell out of here, I'm not sure what I'll do. So much for a beer and some delicious flautas. I can't sit at that table and pretend Peterson's not going to fuck us all over. One thing's for sure. I will *not* go down for the murder of some poor SOB who somehow washed downstream onto Bridger land.

Peterson is out for blood. Bridger blood. He's got the look, and I'm feeling that slimy sensation, like lizards are scrambling beneath my skin.

He's definitely dirty, and he wants to take down Jonathan Bridger. Unlike the mayor, where his beef was personal, this is different. Worse. Since our dad's six feet under, Peterson will settle for us instead. I've seen it in

New York, but I didn't expect to encounter it in Bayfield, Montana.

I crank the engine, listen to the lusty growling of the chrome pipes, kick the bike into gear, and scream out into the evening. I thought my time in Montana was going to be easy. Simple. Boring.

Fuck, was I wrong.

1

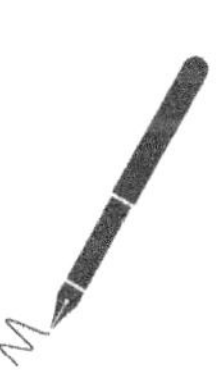

$\mathcal{M}$ILES

I CUT the engine and sigh. Damn, that was a good ride, better here than back home. I yank off my helmet and push my hair back. There's nothing better than straddling a motorcycle and riding the open road.

Here, there's nothing *but* open road. Fucking perfect. It's the best way to clear my head of all the shit going down lately. Not just my asshole father or the stupid rules of his will, but also all the hard labor on the ranch—which I never imagined I'd do in a million years, or for a billion dollars.

The murder, too. Yeah, *murder*, per the pain-in-the-ass detective Peterson.

I left all of that behind at Bridger Ranch.

I climb off my new ride outside of a roadside bar and give it another once over. Yeah, it needs work, but this is what I do. What I live and breathe. Custom builds. All my jobs start off looking like this. Dented. Rusted. Worn. But I see past all that and focus on what it can become.

Not can. *Will.*

The engine is good. All it needs is a little attention. A little babying. A little love. I'll make this motorcycle I found in the bargain bin section of the local paper purr for me, the same way I work a woman.

The sun crawls toward the purple mountains in the distance, but it won't set for another hour or two. I stop just inside the door of the bar. The parking lot is full, so it's popular. The high-top tables and booths skirting both walls are occupied, but the dance floor is empty. Neon signs on the wood-paneled walls give the room a glow of reds and blues. I make my way to the bar and settle on a stool.

The bartender comes over and takes my order, a beer on tap and a burger with fries. I missed the Mexican dinner at the house because of that asshole detective, so I'm hungry. I savor the cool bite of my drink as I wait for the food and then spin around to look over the crowd.

This place is about an hour from Bayfield, so I don't see a familiar face. Not that I expect to recognize anyone.

I've been in the state for two weeks. Not long enough to make friends. I'm just happy to no longer find my brothers a pain in my ass.

I know Carly, Austin's woman. Lexie, the ranch's vet, and most of the ranch staff. Unfortunately, I know Carly's dad, the town mayor, who *is* a pain in the ass. More for Austin than myself, although the man has a pretty big beef with our father that he's carried on to the next generation. Seems to be an unwritten law around here. The sons of Jonathan Bridger are somehow responsible for their father's sins.

Carly herself has helped her dad simmer his shit down, but I doubt we'll be getting a holiday card from him this year. Or ever.

I'll put in my year at Bridger Ranch like the will says, get my billion, and get the hell out of Dodge. In the meantime, I'll enjoy taking out my new ride. At least until it gets cold, which I expect will be sooner than I want.

The music through the hidden speakers changes, and a bunch of screams and hollers have me swiveling on my stool. A group of ladies, clearly having a good time, are partying around two high-tops farther down the bar. They're dressed to go out, which in Montana means jeans, flirty skirts, or dresses with cowboy boots. No stilettos or sequins like I'd see in New York City. No black leather. Hell, I'm the only one wearing that.

One woman has a tiara on her head and a white feathered boa around her neck. A beauty-pageant-style sash is slung over her shoulder and it reads "Soon to be Mrs."

My gaze isn't snagged on the lead bachelorette, but another woman in the group. Why? Because she has her dark eyes on me. I'm not sure she even hears the twang of the country music or sees the dancing and arm waving of her friends. All her attention is squarely on me.

Yeah, *me.*

I raise my brow because if she wants to stare, I don't mind staring right back. She's not hard on the eyes. Far from it. I'd even call her fucking gorgeous. She wears a black tiered miniskirt that flares and hits halfway to her knees. Her top is a plain T-shirt with a deep V that does amazing things to her tits. She's taller than average, and she has meat on her bones. Thick and curvy. A lush body a guy can grip and hang on to. My fingers itch to learn every inch of her.

I'm single, but I'm not a monk. I know when a woman is interested. I can flirt, but I don't like games. Don't like circling. The dance between a man and a woman. I want chemistry. A connection. With those two things, flirting isn't necessary.

With this woman, there's fucking chemistry. I can tell

she feels it too because she's now heading my way. The corner of her full mouth turns up as she sways toward me. I don't look away, not even when the bartender sets my burger on the bar.

Tonight is getting better and better. A good ride on a motorcycle and maybe—most likely—a good ride with a hot woman.

"Hi," she says.

Her voice is deep and husky. Up close, her dark hair is almost black and brushes her shoulders. It's straight and sleek, shiny like the chrome on my custom bikes. She wears makeup, but only a little. She doesn't need fake eyelashes or weird shit done to her eyebrows. She's natural looking, but not like she just came off a weeklong camping trip.

Clearly a woman who wants to look pretty for herself. Not to try to snare a man.

"Hi." I set my feet on the floor and spread my legs so she stands within mine.

She takes the opportunity to step in closer, and I set a hand on her waist. Yeah, all soft curves.

Her lips are full and covered in shiny gloss. Fucking kissable.

She smiles. "I'm Sadie, and I wonder if you can do me a favor."

Hmm... A favor? If it involves those more-than-ahandful tits or any other square inch of her, I'm happy to help.

"Sure."

There is no other answer.

"I'm here with a bachelorette party, which I'm sure is pretty obvious." She thumbs over her shoulder toward the ladies who are making more noise than the rest of the patrons combined.

I offer a nod.

The music changes again and a few people move to the dance floor.

"Part of the fun is to do a dare," she continues.

"A dare?"

She shakes her head, her sleek hair moving like a waterfall over her shoulder. I can't resist brushing the strands back. Yeah, silky soft.

I watch her throat work as she swallows.

"Yeah, I've got to give my panties to a guy."

My eyes meet hers. My dick jerks against my jeans, and I can't help but smile.

"I'll take your panties, sweetheart, but how will they know the dare's been done? I doubt you're going to take them off right here for others to see."

I glance around and then back to her.

Her cheeks turn a pretty shade of pink. Embarrassed now? She was brave enough to come up to a stranger and ask for a favor that involves her panties.

"You have to bring them to the group," she adds.

I slide my thumb back and forth over her waist.

"That's it?"

She nods. "That's it."

I give her a grin. "So you'll go to the ladies' room to take them off...or am I supposed to help you out of them?"

I wouldn't mind helping her out of them. Fuck, yeah.

She bites her lip, lowers her gaze, and then lifts her chin. "I already took them off."

Holy. Shit.

My mouth opens slightly and I reach out and set my beer on the bar, not taking my eyes off her. I pull her in close so I can whisper in her ear. I'm a big guy so even when I'm leaning against the stool, we're at eye level.

"You're not wearing any panties right now?" I whisper.

My dick is completely hard and I shift on the stool to get more comfortable.

She shakes her head and whispers back, "No."

Fuck me.

I pull back, meet her eyes. Her irises are almost all black. Her cheeks are flushed. She licks her lips.

"You drunk?" I ask.

I'm not doing this with a woman who's trashed. What she's asking might be a silly bachelorette party game, but when panties are involved, I like consent every step of the way. No matter what a trashed woman says, there isn't any consent, in my mind.

She shakes her head. "One glass of wine. I have to work tomorrow."

Good.

"So tell me, Sober Sadie. Wouldn't it be a shame to give me your panties and not get anything out of it?"

A little frown forms on her brow. "Oh?"

"You might as well get an orgasm. Right? I mean, you're not wearing any panties. I can just lift that skirt and sink my fingers into your pussy. I bet you're wet, aren't you?"

She hasn't slapped me yet, so I keep on going. I could get into this. My burger is getting cold, but the woman before me is getting hot. I can feel her warmth against my palm. See it with my eyes. If the place weren't potently scented with beer and greasy fries, I could probably even pick up the aroma of her heady arousal.

"Oh my God."

I set my other hand on her waist and pull her in even closer so our centers touch. She can't miss my hard length in my jeans and I can't miss her scalding heat. My pinky fingers curl and lift the back of her skirt an inch or so.

"I'll take those panties," I say, "but I'm a giver. Want to come on my fingers in return?"

2

*S*ADIE

"I DON'T EVEN KNOW your name," I tell him, not able to tear my eyes away.

He's gorgeous. And direct. And wants to give me an orgasm.

"Miles."

His sandy colored hair has a slight curl and because it's a little long on top, it falls over his forehead. His eyes are also fair, but still piercing. He's tan as if he's been in the sun, but he's not a California surfer or a farmer, and he's definitely not a Stetson-wearing cowboy like most of the men around here. Not with his dark denim and snug

T-shirt. None of that hides his height—even sitting down —or his sturdy build. A few tattoos circle his well-defined biceps, but it's the motorcycle helmet on the stool beside him that indicates he might be a bit of a bad boy.

In my line of work, I put those kinds behind bars. Profiling? Hell, yes. Especially when the guy offers to finger me for pleasure. At a bar.

Maybe I should flash him the badge I have in my purse. Or tell him to fuck off with his cheesy, over-the-top shit that guys usually spew with the hope of getting laid.

He doesn't mention his dick coming out though. Only that he wants to put his hand up my skirt.

Am I thinking about his offer?

Yes. Is it stupid?

Maybe.

Before I became a detective, I went on enough calls involving various kinds of assaults against women. None of them good. Yet I'm still thinking about his words.

Maybe I'm horny.

There's no *maybe* about it. I am.

Nothing wrong with that. I'm in a dry spell and not one guy in the county—and I know pretty much all of them—does it for me. It's not as if hot men grow like alfalfa or wheat around here.

I'm impressed that he asked about how much I had to drink. The bachelorette party is for my friend Tracy, who's getting married in two weeks. While we've been here for an hour, everyone started drinking at Tracy's house a few hours ago. There's a limo to take us around, but I might as well be the designated driver. I've been sipping wine since I'm on shift tomorrow. With a probable murder added to my usual case load, I can't be hungover. Not with that stickler Mark as my partner.

Inwardly, I roll my eyes thinking about him in comparison to Miles. The hot guy who I picked to do the stupid dare.

Miles wants me to remember him touching me.

"You do this all the time?" I ask.

"Stop at a bar for a burger and a beer? If I can get on my bike for a ride, yeah."

I glance at his helmet again. He's hot *and* smart, putting a brain bucket on instead of having his head scraped across the pavement for my colleagues to clean up.

"I meant...exchange *favors*."

A smile tugs at his lips. Very kissable lips. He's got whiskers that I bet would feel especially nice on the insides of my thighs.

I squirm a little. The idea makes me wet. The quirk of his mouth turns into a full-on grin. My cheeks heat. The feel of his hands on my waist is non-threatening. Light.

But I can feel how big they are, how warm he is. I wouldn't mind being a little manhandled.

"I can say I've never been asked to take a woman's panties and then return them to her friends." He lifts his eyebrows. "I'd rather keep them."

"Got a big collection?" I ask, not sure if I want the answer.

"I don't kiss and tell. Remember, sweetheart, you approached *me*."

Good answer.

I bite my lip and consider. As I do, he pulls me in, and swivels on his stool so he's facing the bar and I'm between it and his front. I'm trapped with his bent legs on either side of me, but in the middle of a busy bar. We're not alone. In my periphery, I can see the bartender moving back and forth getting drinks. While the stools on either side of us are empty, there are people at the bar. At the high tops. Everywhere.

He hasn't looked away from me yet. "You want to give me those panties now?"

I blink and reach into my cross-body purse. They're stuffed on top, and I pull them out but keep them low between us. I don't need to flash them to everyone in the bar.

My pussy's bare beneath my skirt, and every time I

move I can't forget. I've never, *ever* gone commando before.

He takes them, the lavender lace looking delicate in his big hand. Calluses line his palm. Clearly he works hard.

He stares at the panties. "This little scrap's all that covered you? Not much better than going bare."

Leaning back a little, he tucks them into the front pocket of his jeans before setting his hands on my thighs over my skirt. "I'll take these over to your friends." He tips his head in their direction.

I glance toward our tables, but the girls have moved to the dance floor and are doing a line dance.

"First, how about I make you feel good?"

I shift my gaze back to his. "Here?"

We're right in the middle of the bar.

He slides his hands down the outside of my legs until he's touching my bare skin. Then he changes direction and works his way right back up. He doesn't lift the skirt, but it catches on his hands so it covers them.

"No one can see," he says. "Even with me sitting, we're eye level. No one knows I've got my fingers a few inches from your pussy."

My mouth opens and closes like a fish. Oh my God.

Here?

Now?

Yes, he's definitely going to touch me here and now.

"I can't come in front of all these people," I whisper.

He leans in close and slides his nose up my neck, nuzzling. "I like how you know I'll be able to get you to come. With just my fingers. Right here."

My skin warms, and goose bumps rise across my arms. I jolt when a finger brushes over my folds.

"Shh," he whispers directly in my ear.

"Miles, I can't...I mean—"

"Every guy in here wishes he were me. Touching the prettiest woman in the place. Fuck, you're drenched."

Yeah, he can't miss my reaction to him. Why I'm so wet for a guy who's touching me in a room full of people, I have no idea.

"What else might you like? How about this?" He pulls back enough so our eyes meet.

A finger sinks into me.

I gasp.

"Sadie!"

I jolt at Tracy's voice.

Miles's finger falls away, and I whimper at the loss. I'm close to coming just from that little bit of contact. Is it the man? The ridiculously naughty way he was touching my body, yet keeping what we were doing hidden? Right at the bar?

Tracy comes up in a very buzzed rush of white boa feathers and giggles. "Come dance!"

I look to Miles, who's smiling. His hands fall away completely and I watch—mortified—as he lifts the finger he just had inside me to his lips. And sucks.

"Did she give you her panties?" Tracy practically shouts.

I whip my head around to see if anyone notices. Yeah, I'm more embarrassed by that than by the way Miles had his hands up my skirt.

"She did," he replies, amusement lacing his words.

He pulls them from his pocket to show Tracy, who squeals.

"Come dance!" she calls to me.

Miles shifts so I can be pulled away by Tracy. I glance at him and offer him a little wave as I'm tugged onto the dance floor and into the middle of the group of women. By the time the song is over and I look back, Miles is gone. And so are my panties. Tracy never snagged them.

Disappointment follows me the rest of the night. Being the only sober one at a bachelorette party isn't all that great to start with, but then to be yanked away from an oncoming orgasm? Cruel.

Once at home and in bed, I toss and turn all night, dreaming of the sexy biker and his talented fingers, knowing the only way I'm getting orgasms anytime soon is with my vibrator.

Guys like Miles don't exist in the area. And he said he was on a motorcycle ride. A ride that probably took him right back out of the county and to some other lucky girl.

3

M ILES

"THIS IS A PAIN IN MY ASS," Chance grumbles, dirt kicking up beneath the heels of his worn work boots. "Why the hell do we need to be questioned again? He was here last night."

We make our way along the narrow dirt road between the main house and one of the many outbuildings on the vast Bridger property. The one we came from houses the ATVs and other mechanical equipment—tractors, snowmobiles, and even a snowplow. The space is big, well-kept, and more importantly, heated. My dream mechanic's shop. If I'm staying here for a year, I figure I can use the space for my custom jobs.

I might have to follow the constraints of our dead father's will and take up ranching in the middle of Bumfuck, Montana, but it doesn't mean I can't keep my business going in my downtime. MB Custom Builds can continue from anywhere, as long as I have room to work —which I do—and my clients ship their bikes or cars here instead of to my shop in New York. In the meantime, I'll enjoy working on the older bike I just bought.

"The body might have been on our land, but the police have nothing to tie us to the murder," Austin says. "*If* what Peterson says is true."

The way Austin says *our* land doesn't go unnoticed. A shit ton has happened in the short time we've been here, and I agree with Austin. This place, even the stupid cows, feels more and more like...ours.

"Easy for you to say," Chance counters. "You just got here. I have no alibi unless the police can pinpoint exactly *when* the man was killed. Even then, I might not have one."

Chance's face is shaded from the bright sun by his Stetson, which he pretty much always wears unless he's driving. I assume he takes it off for the shower and to sleep, but we aren't close enough for me to know for sure.

He has a point.

"Louisa didn't say anything about the police bringing a warrant this time," I say, hoping that will ease his mind. "They're not going to be poking around."

The housekeeper called Chance's cell to notify us of the unexpected visitors.

The local police. Again.

We come up around the back side of the house.

"It's got to be because of Jonathan," I say. "Who else was that big of an asshole? I never even met the guy, but I wouldn't put murder past him."

We turn the corner and proceed along the paved walkway, flanked by gardener-maintained flower beds, until we reach the steps leading to the front porch.

Two people hop up from the rocking chairs and I halt in my tracks.

"Oh, shit," I mutter, eyeing one of them.

The one I know. Very well.

Intimately, in fact.

Out of all the bars in all of Montana, I stopped at the one where *she* was for a bachelorette party. Fuck. *Fuck!*

"Peterson, what now?" Chance demands.

Out of the corner of my eye, I see Chance cross his arms over his chest. I don't look away from...*her*.

From Sadie.

"Brought my partner today," Peterson says. "Sadie Hopkins."

Unlike the night before, when she was in an easily-liftable skirt, Sadie is now in jeans and a white blouse with a few modest buttons undone exposing the cotton of a tank top—no cleavage in sight. Her hair, which was silky soft between my fingers, is pulled back in a low ponytail. She has a gun in a holster at her hip along with a shiny badge clipped to her leather belt. I sure as hell find it sexy, comparing the woman from the night before to the one standing in front of me.

I don't see any handcuffs on her belt, but I wouldn't mind her pulling them out for a little fun.

Although... She might be more motivated to put them on me or one of my brothers for a less pleasant reason.

Murder.

Her dark eyes are wide and her full lips—which I wish I had sampled—are in a thin line.

She doesn't say a word.

At least her name really *is* Sadie. At the bar, I shared mine with her but nothing else. Not because I wanted it to be a secret. We didn't talk about our jobs. We didn't talk about anything except how her party friends were expected to do something daring—in her case, to give a man her panties.

And she chose me.

The second our eyes connected—yeah, it sounds corny as fuck—but the ridiculous chemistry between us was insane. My dick was hard when she was pulled off my finger and onto the dance floor. It was hard all the way back to the ranch and only went down when I rubbed one out in the shower. And then only for a short time because I couldn't stop thinking about her.

Now, I'm instantly hard all over again.

Fuck, I feel the pull now, like a living thing between us. My heart pounds and my dick throbs. My fingers itch to brush over her soft skin, to get back inside her pussy and give her that orgasm we were both denied.

"Austin Bridger."

I have to snap out of my stare or I'm going to get both of us in big fucking trouble.

I have no intention of letting anyone know I had my hands on one of the police officers investigating the death on the ranch. That I know how she looks when she's aroused, that she makes a little whimper when my finger's in her pussy. That she doesn't mind a little exhibitionism. I'm not a sharer, but that was hot as hell.

What we did on our own time—even in front of an entire bar—isn't for anyone else to know about. I don't kiss and tell or ruin someone's career by being an asshole. Especially if I'm interested in a potential round two.

I pull my head out of my ass and offer her my hand. "Miles."

She nods and a pretty flush spreads across her cheeks.

Peterson clears his throat. "Any chance we can go inside and sit down? It's a hot day."

Chance tenses.

"The porch is nice and shady," I offer. "After a morning counting calves, this'll be a nice break."

No way is Peterson getting in the house to look around without a warrant. And I need a little time to come to terms with Sadie from the bar being Sadie, the detective.

I still want her in my bed, preferably naked and without her badge, gun, and warrant.

Peterson's jaw clenches, but he returns to the rocker he vacated when we came up.

Sadie still hasn't said a word. She leans against the porch railing, forgoing a seat.

Chance settles on the opposite end of the railing, resting his hip against the post, while Austin takes the vacant seat.

I take the opportunity to stand beside Sadie so it's easy to see everyone. And to pick up her floral scent, which dredges up memories of the night before.

"Any idea who the victim is?" I ask Sadie.

Her gaze holds mine for a moment and then she blinks. "None yet. The body was sent to the coroner in Missoula."

"Do you have an idea who it might be?" Peterson asks.

"You three were at the creek the day before the body was found."

I look away from Sadie and to the jerk who not-so-subtly insinuates we killed a man.

"We went over this already with you, Officer," Chance says through clenched teeth.

"*Detective*," Peterson corrects. "You could have killed the man and no one would have found him for weeks. Months, if ever. That stretch of creek is pretty isolated."

I frown at the absurdity. "And like we said last night, *why* would we kill the guy, dump him in the creek, and then break up the beaver dam so the water would go down and he'd be discovered? I'm no detective, *Detective*, but that makes zero sense."

I don't like this fucker any more today than I did last night.

"My woman found the body." Austin's voice is deep, almost a growl. "Tripped over it. You think I'd subject her to something like that?"

Austin and Carly have gotten close fast. I like her. She seems to be coming into herself with him. Seems to be in his nature to take care of people, like he does for his mom.

"We're reviewing the employees of the ranch, ruling them out one by one," Sadie says.

Her voice is soft and almost velvety. Just as I remember.

"We're more interested in your father because, well... he's dead. We can't interview a dead man," she adds.

Chance stands. "My father's lawyer is Tom Shankle. Talk to him."

"We want to hear about him from you," Peterson replies.

Chance turns, sets his hands on his hips. "If I were going to commit murder, I'd have done it already." He holds up his hand. "And no, it wouldn't have been the man in the creek. I'd have killed my father. And I'd have been justified in doing so."

"Sounds like you're telling me you have violent thoughts," Peterson pushes.

"About Jonathan Bridger. That's all I've got left when it comes to him. If you want to put this murder on me, you're wasting your time, but have at it." Chance removes his hat, swipes a hand over his hair, and sets it back on his head. "Got work to do."

He walks off and I can't help but grin. Yeah, he has big fucking balls since he pretty much gave the lead detective the middle finger.

I glance at Sadie, who has her lower lip gripped between her teeth. Speaking of giving someone the finger...

Austin stands. "Anything else?"

Peterson rises, adjusts his belt. "That's all. For now."

He sets off toward the sheriff SUV parked in the driveway.

Austin nods to Sadie, and heads inside, the oversized entry door clicking shut behind him.

I turn to face Sadie full-on, tuck my thumbs in my jeans pocket so I don't reach out and touch her.

"Miles *Bridger.* I didn't know who you were." She rubs her hands over her jean-clad thighs. "What are the odds I'd pick *you?* God, I should've just gone with one of the farmers."

Hell, no. A fucking farmer?

"You look angry." She rakes her gaze over my face and settles on my mouth.

I shake my head. "The idea of any other guy at that bar getting his hands on you makes me pretty mad."

Her lips form an O.

"I didn't think I'd see you again, but I admit, I'm pretty pleased." I glance over her shoulder.

Peterson is leaning against the SUV, typing something into his cell. He's not watching us, so I figure we have a little time.

"That I gave one of the prime suspects in the murder I'm investigating my panties?"

I grin and can't help but slide my finger down her skin from the base of her throat to the curved edge of her tank top. She sucks in a breath and her breasts swell beneath her blouse.

"You gave me more than your panties," I murmur.

"You were supposed to give them back," she snaps, her cheeks turning a pretty pink.

Oh, she has fire. I shake my head. "Your friend didn't take them, and now, I have no intention of giving them back. Maybe I'll consider it, though, if you go out with me."

Her eyes widen. "So I can give you another pair?"

"I don't need to go out with you for that."

She steps back and crosses her arms over her chest. Fuck, she's hot when she's riled. Especially now that I know who she is. That I'm *definitely* going to see her again. Even if it's only in an official capacity since it seems the Bridger brothers are prime suspects, at least in her partner's eyes.

"I want to go out with you to get to know you," I admit. "More than your name. More than how you feel beneath my palms in a room full of people."

"I'd lose my job. Dating a suspect is a bad career move."

"Clear me. No conflict of interest then."

"Not happening." She glances over her shoulder. "Fair warning, Peterson's got a hard-on for the three of you. He sees this case as a way to advance his career. Pinning the murder on one of the billionaire Bridgers."

"And yours?"

Maybe she knew about me after all and approached me at the bar specifically. She could have gone to any guy with her silly bachelorette game. She picked me. Why?

She shrugs her slim shoulders. "I follow the evidence. It doesn't lead to you, and that was clear before I knew who you were."

She jumps at the blare of a car horn.

"Nice guy," I say. "Came all the way out here twice just to let us know he doesn't like us."

She nods. "I've got to go."

She ambles down the steps as I watch.

"See you around, Sadie."

She slows but keeps on going.

Yeah, I'll be seeing her around. In my bed. On the back of my bike. Anywhere I can get her.

The little fun we had at the bar isn't enough. I want more. I want to know everything about Sadie. The woman. As for her being a detective on the murder case? Keeping her close doesn't hurt there either.

As I watch the SUV drive off, I think about her partner. I might want to get to know everything about him as well, before I find myself—or one of my brothers—behind bars.

Permanently.

4
____

MARK STARES AHEAD at the road, his lips pursed. I can tell he's ready to say something I'm not going to like. I know the look on his face.

He clears his throat. Finally. "Do you know that Bridger fellow? Miles?"

I play it cool because...well, several reasons. One, I don't share my personal life with Mark. Ever. He's my partner, but he's not my friend. In fact, he's a dick. Two, if he finds out I have any kind of connection with Miles, he'll either use it to his advantage or use it to fuck me over. I'd expect both from him.

So I lie. "No. Do you?"

"He was looking at you with"—another throat clear —"what *appeared* to be recognition."

Peterson sometimes likes to think he's a father figure to me, which is weird because he's not much older than I am and he also likes to stare at my chest, which makes the first part creepy as hell. He's a decent detective when he goes by the book, but he's definitely got an unsettling side.

"How could I know either one of them?" I ask. "They moved here yesterday."

"It was a couple weeks ago, I think." Peterson stops the car at the red light at Broad and Main, near the station.

"I was being hyperbolic, Mark." I sigh. "My point is that Miles and Austin Bridger recently came to Bayfield for the first time, and from what I hear, their father left them with a huge mess with that will of his."

News of their arrival and the reason behind it spread across the county like wildfire.

"Not to mention a dead body." Peterson lurches the SUV forward when the light turns green and he pulls in front of the station—right in front of a fire hydrant.

He always does that, even when he could pull up a few feet and leave the hydrant free. Peterson's the kind of cop who takes all the liberties granted him.

Pisses me off.

But I'm a rookie, and I have to work with someone. It

may as well be a seasoned detective like Peterson. He does know his stuff...when he keeps to the book.

"What's your beef with the Bridgers, anyway?" I ask once we're back in the station.

"Who says I have any beef with them?" He glances at his phone.

I give him a perturbed look he doesn't pick up on. "You couldn't have made your feelings clearer. I mean, you went out there twice just to mess with them. We haven't even heard back from the coroner yet. Those three—at least the two newcomers, for sure—obviously had nothing to do with that dead body. And I've known Chance Bridger since I moved here over a year ago. He's a decent man."

Mark gives me a patronizing look as he grabs his dirty coffee mug off his desk. "Listen, Hopkins. You're a good cop, but you've got a lot to learn. When you've been doing this as long as I have, you learn to trust your instinct. And my instinct is telling me those boys know more than they're letting on."

Boys? Chance Bridger has to be around thirty, and I'd bet his brothers are older.

"Stick with me," Peterson continues. "I'll teach you how to ferret out evidence in the most unlikely places."

I grit my teeth to keep from telling him the unlikely place where I want him to stick something.

"You know I appreciate your guidance," I say. "But *my* instinct is telling me the Bridger brothers are innocent."

"Your instinct is non-existent," Peterson says. "No rookie a year out of the academy knows anything."

I hold back a scoff. "I guess I knew enough to get hired as a detective after only a year in uniform."

He doesn't reply because his phone buzzes. He puts it to his ear. "Peterson."

I walk to my desk when the receptionist calls to me from her spot by the door. "Sadie, you've got a call on line one."

I frown and stare down at the phone on my desk. "I do?"

"You sure do," she calls.

Strange. No one calls me on the landline. We all use our cells. I pick up the receiver. "This is Hopkins."

"Hey, Hopkins. This is Bridger."

My heart nearly flips out of my chest.

Sure, he told me who he was, but I'd know that deep, rich voice anywhere. It belongs to the man whose finger made me insane last night.

The man my partner seems determined to put behind bars.

"What do you want?" I ask, a little more harshly than I mean to.

"Easy." He laughs. "I don't know your cell number, but

all it took was a quick search to find the number for the local sheriff's office. How'd you like to have dinner with me tonight?"

My flesh prickles and my pussy clenches as I recall how skillfully he touched me in a room full of people.

I glance to Peterson, who's not looking in my direction. God, yes, I'd like to have dinner with Miles. Better yet, I'd like to skip dinner and get under him because if he's as talented as he was with just his fingers, I know it'll be amazing when he gives me his all. Meaning his dick and mouth too.

But it can't happen. Not while I'm investigating a dead body found on his land. Last night was a mistake. Innocent, yes, and I could explain it away as an epic coincidence. But a second time?

"You know I can't," I say finally.

"What? You can ride my fingers in the middle of a bar but you can't have dinner with me?"

God, my cheeks are on fire. That gruff voice does things to me. Damn it.

"Besides," he continues, "don't you want those pretty lace panties back?"

"I thought you said I wasn't going to get them back."

He laughs. "I said I'd consider returning them if you go out with me. Of course I'm happy to keep them as a souvenir. They smell like you."

God. He's a dirty talker. And he's skilled. *And* he's uninhibited. Why do his words make me want to explode all over his fingers? Because it never happened. I got close and then we were interrupted. I want more than what we did the night before. I want to take his dick for a spin. I'm betting it's magnificent. And huge. He has to be proportional, right?

"You going to say something this century?" he asks.

I lick my dry lips and then turn away from Peterson and everyone else in the station. "Miles—"

"Tell you what," he says, cutting me off. "We'll go back to Silverton. Or somewhere even farther from Bayfield. No one will see you cavorting with a murder suspect."

I sigh. "I don't think you or your brothers had anything to do with that body."

"But your partner does."

"Yeah. I haven't lived here that long, but apparently your old man had a lot of enemies."

"I might have his DNA, but I never met the man. Never talked to him. Yet I've been here less than two weeks and I've already met several people who hate his guts, and mine now too. I'm betting that dead guy hated him, too."

"Most likely, but it's my job to prove it."

Silence for a moment, until—

"I'm aging here, Hopkins. I don't give a shit about the investigation, as long as it steers away from me and my brothers. I want more of you. *You.* Not your badge. Although...you can bring the handcuffs."

I close my eyes, draw in a breath, and can't help but smile. "Okay. Just dinner. And somewhere...not here."

"You choose the place. I don't know the area very well yet."

"There's a cute little Italian place in Silverton. I'll have to meet you there. Around seven?"

"Hell, no," he replies. "When I take a gorgeous woman out, I pick her up."

I sigh again. I normally hate pushy, but for some reason, it feels good with him. He's being chivalrous. Manly. After hanging out with Peterson at work, a real man is what I need. "Okay. But not at work. I'll meet you outside Millie's at six-thirty."

"All right. But you better be in disguise. You wouldn't want anyone to see you get into a car with the notorious criminal Miles Bridger."

Shit. "Right. I'm not thinking."

"You could give me your address, you know. That'd make this a lot easier."

I could. But I'm a cop. I know better than to give out my address to someone I just met—especially a suspect in an investigation, even if I *do* think he's innocent.

Someone I just met who had me on the brink of an orgasm last night in a public place...

Instinct.

Peterson made a big deal about instinct.

He may think I have none, but he's dead wrong. I've relied on instinct my whole life, and I won't let some cowboy cop convince me I don't have any.

My instinct tells me the Bridgers are innocent, and it also tells me I have nothing to fear from Miles. I mean, what's the difference between getting into a car with him at Millie's and getting into a car with him at my place? He might be a stranger to me, but he's infamous in town. From what I've heard about the will, he's not going anywhere for a year.

Regardless, he'll know where I live.

"Fine. Six-thirty." I share my address. "It's an old house converted into three apartments."

"Good girl. Six-thirty it is. Wear the skirt from last night."

I frown. "Why?"

"You looked hot as hell in it."

I don't reply. I'm too busy squirming against the tickle between my legs.

"Hey Sadie?"

"Yeah?"

"I can't fucking wait."

MILES LOOKS like he could be on the cover of a magazine. Some outdoorsy fitness magazine. Not the kind where he's climbing a mountain, but a gorgeous guy who works out in some underground urban gym with thick ropes to climb, huge tires to flip, and plenty of weights to lift.

He shows up at my place in dark jeans and a black button down that contrasts stunningly with his light hair and eyes. The sleeves are rolled up about halfway to his elbows, and his forearms are corded and sexy. I need to get a better look at those tattoos, too.

And his hands. I didn't get a good look at them in the dim lighting of the bar the night before, but I felt them. They're big and strong and perfectly shaped.

God, those long, thick fingers...

One of which was inside me last night...

Already I'm feeling the anticipation between my legs.

"You look beautiful." He steps close and pushes a strand of hair behind my ear.

Goose bumps skitter across my flesh. "Thank you. You look great too."

"Don't make me blush." He smiles and...*shit*, a dimple appears. "Shall we?"

I'm a curvy woman, but Miles Bridger makes me feel almost petite. He's got to be six-five at least, and his shoulders are broad and beefy. I'm the one in law enforcement, the one who does the protecting, but right now, I feel... feminine. Small. Protected.

He takes my elbow and leads me down the front walk. He opens the passenger door for me and I step up into the huge truck. I know it belongs to the Bridger Ranch, not only because I've reviewed their vehicle registrations as part of my investigation, but because there's no way Miles would buy a truck like this. I picture him in a sleek Jaguar or a muscle car.

"No bike?" I ask as he pulls away from the curb.

He glances over at me, raking his gaze down my body. "Can't wear that skirt on the back of a bike. If anything's going into your panties tonight, it's going to be me."

Oh. My. God. I smooth the short hem. My cheeks heat when he chuckles.

I don't say anything as he makes his way out of town. Once we're on the road toward Silverton, he turns on some jazz.

"I love jazz," I tell him, thankful for a topic other than my panties.

"Do you? Me too."

I fidget a little. "So what do you do? I mean, for a job. At home. New York, right?"

Great, I'm babbling.

"Yes. New York. I build custom bikes. Sometimes cars,

but mostly bikes. I've got my own business, but something tells me you already know this."

Busted. "I know the basics from my investigation, nothing else."

"I figure you know my blood type and dick size," he murmurs.

I gasp and whip my head his way.

He's smirking. "B negative, and you can measure the other thing yourself later."

"Confident much?"

He reaches out, leaving one hand on the wheel, to run his knuckles down my cheek. "Sweetheart, I had my fingers in your pussy last night. While I never take what's not willingly offered, I have a good feeling about you and me and later tonight."

He's probably right. No, *definitely* right. No guy I've ever met in Montana is like Miles. Direct. Straightforward. I'm not saying local guys don't want sex, but he's...different.

"What about the bike you rode last night?" I ask.

"Bought that the other day. I'll work on it and make her shine again, on top of projects from clients. I've got a bike in transit right now for one of my regulars." He laughs. "You know the type. Rich investment bankers who like to pretend they're bikers on the weekends."

I join him in laughter.

He rests his arm on the center console, the tips of his fingers brushing my thigh. "But hey, I love the work, and these guys love their toys. I'm lucky I can do what I love for people who can afford to pay me for it."

I look him over. "You don't seem like a mechanic."

"Oh?"

"Yeah. Your hands are too clean."

He laughs again. "I wear latex gloves. The real mess is when I'm with my brothers. You should have seen them after Austin, Chance, and I broke up that dam on the property. I looked worse than the greasiest day in my shop. Besides the gloves, they make special soap for mechanics, Hopkins."

"Right."

I knew that of course. I'm babbling again. Clean hands. God.

"How'd you become a detective?" he asks. "Nancy Drew books?"

I have to smile that a big, rugged guy like him knows about one of my favorite childhood book series.

"It's kind of a long story."

He tears his gaze from the road and glances my way. "We've got a twenty-minute drive."

I don't talk about my decision a lot. It's too painful and

brings up so many regrets. But for some reason, I want to tell Miles. For him to understand me.

"You're probably expecting me to say that one of my parents was a cop or something. That's how most people get into it. But my mom is a hairdresser and my dad owns a construction company in Billings. They're divorced."

God, Sadie, stop with the babbling already! He asked why you became a cop, not for your parents' life stories.

"So it wasn't some kind of family legacy," he says.

"No. I went to two years of college. My grades were good, but it wasn't my thing. I couldn't decide what I wanted to study, and then, about three years ago, my brother disappeared."

Miles looks my way, his jaw clenching. Those fingertips that had been brushing my leg settle on it, give a little squeeze. "My God. I'm so sorry, Sadie."

I shrug and look out the passenger window. "We weren't that close. He was ten years older and was estranged from my mom and me. I was a little kid when he left home and rarely saw him. Anyway, the investigation trail dried up quickly."

He reaches and turns the radio down slightly. "Wait. Are you saying your brother was murdered?"

I sigh. "We don't really know. They never found a body and all investigations were called off within a month of his disappearance. He was hauling freight across the Canadian border last anyone heard, so it's possible he decided to stay in Canada, make a new life, but...*why* would he do that? Staying in Canada wouldn't be so bad, but why not reach out to us?"

"Jesus..."

I clear my throat. "Anyway, even though I didn't really know my brother anymore, the whole thing got me interested in law enforcement, and specifically detective work. I felt like there was something more that the guys on my brother's case weren't seeing. So I enrolled in the police academy and somehow I ended up here in Bayfield. I originally thought I'd join the force in Billings, but there was an opening here, and I got it."

"You're young for a detective," he comments.

"I'm twenty-eight. I was only in uniform for a year before they promoted me."

"That's pretty impressive."

I'm not sure how to reply, so I simply keep talking. "Not that there's a ton of detective work to do in such a small town, which is probably why the Bridger investigation is such a wet dream for Peterson. He's itching to solve a murder case."

"I hope he solves it," Miles says. "Because when he does, he'll prove that my brothers and I are innocent."

We hit the Silverton town limits. "Rigazzi's is just up there on your right." I point toward the restaurant. "There are a few parking spaces in the back. It's a weeknight, so you might get lucky."

"Oh, I'll get lucky." He grins. "I always do."

He might be a little cocky, but he's probably not wrong.

5

$\mathcal{M}$ILES

WHEN I TOOK the keys for one of the ranch's trucks, Chance didn't ask where I was going or what I was doing. Maybe it's because we spent all day together tracking a bunch of calves, or maybe because we're grown fucking men. He lifted his chin at me on my way out the door and nothing more.

I had no intention of telling him that I'm taking Sadie out for dinner. He probably wouldn't care because hell, she can give us the inside scoop on what the hell's going on with the dead body. Feeding a detective might mean she feeds us info right back. Not that I'm going to fuck the detective for information.

Oh, I'll fuck Sadie for sure, but not because of the case.

I might be a dick sometimes, but I'm not an asshole. And not to women.

Especially not to Sadie because there's something about her. Something besides the hot, wet clench of her pussy around my fingers or her calm demeanor that hides her passionate—and what I figure is a little naughty—nature.

It was a painful ride home. Sitting astride a motorcycle with a raging hard on is far from fun. Once I got back I took care of things in the shower. It didn't take long since I had the scent of her on my fingers and her panties in my pocket.

I never expected to see her again, which didn't sit well with me. There was a connection. There had to be—she gave me her panties and let me under her skirt in the middle of a bar. Sadie isn't the kind of woman who routinely lets a random guy finger her in a public place. Not sure how I know this, but I do.

After my initial surprise when she showed up at the house, I was happy to see her. So was my dick. I didn't even wait two hours after she rode away with her prick of a partner before I tracked her down at the station and asked her out.

I don't do relationships. I never wanted to. I always figured I was too fucked up. But I never found a woman who hooks me like Sadie does. I want to know everything about her, including stories like her missing brother. It affected her deeply. So deeply she chose her career because of it.

The hostess leads us through the restaurant to a high-backed booth, one near a server station toward the front. When she sets the menus on the table, I point out another one farther down the wall of windows. With a hand at the small of Sadie's back, I follow the hostess to the better spot. Quieter. More private.

Instead of taking the seat across from her, I settle my big frame beside Sadie after she slides in. She scoots over with a little laugh.

"There's a whole other side, big guy."

I shake my head and slide a menu in front of her. "Too far."

She offers me a playful eye roll but doesn't say anything else. This close, I can see flecks of gold in her brown irises. She has a little mole beside her right eye.

"What?" she asks, when I keep looking at her.

"Can't a guy look at the prettiest thing in the room?"

A flush spreads across her cheeks and down her neck

as she drops her gaze to the menu on the checkered table-cloth. I wonder how far that color goes.

I'm not lying. She *is* the prettiest thing in the restaurant. She's the prettiest woman I've seen in a while. I would normally sit across from a date, civilized and all, but there's something about Sadie that pushes me to be closer. To want more. To get inside her. And not just her pussy.

I'd take her across the table if I could, but I can wait. I have no choice.

"What are you getting?" I ask after we study the options.

"Chicken piccata," she replies.

The server drops off waters and a basket of bread. I give both our orders, and she departs.

"I can order for myself." Sadie tilts her head to look at me.

I shrug and set my arm along the back of the booth so my fingers brush her shoulder. "I like taking care of you."

"You don't even know me," she replies.

"I want to," I admit. "Tell me a secret."

She laughs. "A secret?"

I nod. "Something no one else knows."

"I...don't like eggs." She actually shivers in disgust admitting that.

"That can't be a secret," I counter. "Your parents must know."

She nods. "My mom does, but she doesn't believe me that it's a thing. I mean, who hates eggs? So she served them anyway and made me eat them. I put tons of jelly on top to get them down."

I frown at the disgusting idea of eggs mixed with jelly and then reach out and slide a finger through her silky hair. It's long and sticks straight to her shoulders. "No eggs. Got it."

"What about you?" She tilts her head again.

I'm not sure if she realizes she's done it, making room for my finger to brush down her neck.

"I've never done this before."

She shifts in her seat to face me head-on and my touch falls away. I set it on her thigh, my palm on her skirt but my fingertips flirting with the short hem.

"Eaten dinner? Dated?" She laughs. "I can't believe that. The guy I met last night was no virgin."

A smile tugs at my lips. "Don't worry. I know what I'm doing."

She licks her lips and her pink tongue flicks out. Damn.

"I've never...been with a woman I'm interested in keeping."

She blinks. "Keeping?"

I shrug. "No woman's ever handed me her panties before."

Which, of course, isn't the reason I'm interested in keeping Sadie, but this is all new to me. I'm not sure exactly what to say.

The waitress delivers Sadie's glass of red wine and she waits until the woman leaves before she speaks.

"That was a game for a bachelorette party. You can't tell me guys don't do dares or stupid things at bachelor parties."

I scratch my temple. "All we do is see how trashed we can all get while ogling strippers. I liked the panty thing a hell of a lot better."

"I bet you did." She takes a sip of wine. "The panty thing isn't a secret, though. I was there. I know about it."

I study her, all light and bright and sweet. I want to mess her up so fucking bad. Get those lips swollen, see if her nipples match the color of her blush. Hell, I wonder if her pussy is just as pink.

"I said I've never done this before. *That's* a secret. I've never wanted a woman in my bed so bad before. I've never wanted to keep her there. My secret is most of the women I've been with have been flings."

"Fuck 'em and forget 'em," she says.

"Not as crude as that. I respect women. Appreciate

their wants and desires as much as mine, but never more than once."

"But I'm different?" she whispers.

I lean in close, kiss her forehead. "I'm not sure if I'll ever get enough."

It's the truth. and not only did I reveal this to Sadie, but to myself as well.

The waitress brings our meals and we chat about anything and everything. Football, Montana winters, food options in New York, favorite vacations.

Sadie excuses herself to the ladies' room as I pay the check. I wait for her.

Ten minutes pass. She should be back by now.

I cut through the restaurant to the bathrooms.

I halt at the start of the back hallway. Sadie's standing there, a guy crowding her in.

"Come on, a pretty lady like you?" the man says, his voice slurred.

I see red. The guy's crowding her into the wall and she seems so small and fragile trapped by the big guy.

"Step back, please." Her voice is loud and clear.

It's not a tone of voice she uses with me. More authoritarian, like a teacher or a...yeah, a law enforcement officer. But she's not wearing a uniform and she doesn't have her gun or badge at her hip. Tonight she's just a woman.

My woman. She's with me, and she's mine to protect.

I don't wait a second longer to intervene.

I approach, slap the man on the shoulder.

"Hey! What's—"

"Thanks for keeping my girl company for me," I say. "But I think she just told you to step back."

I want to bash his nose in and toss the guy behind a dumpster, but this is small-town life and I want to be welcomed back to the restaurant. I also don't want to taint our date with violence or anything that might involve paperwork on Sadie's part.

"Wha—"

I tug and he steps back. Sadie steps away and I wrap my arm around her. While the guy might tower over Sadie, I tower over *him*. He has to tip his head back to meet my gaze. His bloodshot eyes widen, and he swallows. *Yeah, you fucked with the wrong woman, asshole.*

"It means a lot to me that you're watching out for her. I don't want any creepers fucking with her, being pushy and not taking no for an answer. You know what I mean?"

He bobs his head.

I slap him on the shoulder once more, this time with a hell of a lot more force. He stumbles into the wall and since he's drunk, hits face first. A framed photo of what I assume is historic Montana rattles.

"You good, sweetheart?" I ask.

She looks up at me and nods. I take her hand and

steer her out of the restaurant. Once out on the sidewalk, she turns and faces me, our hands still locked together.

"Thanks for taking care of me," she says. "I wasn't interested in arresting someone tonight."

I lean down, look in her eyes to see that she really is okay. She's not shaking or upset. She's solid. "It's my job to take care of you, sweetheart."

Her face lights up as she smiles. I have to wonder if anyone ever takes care of her. It's a fucking shame if she doesn't know what it's like to have a man watch out for her.

"But I haven't taken care of you yet." I lower my voice and kiss her. I can't wait any longer. The closeness of the dinner, the fact that another man had been skeeving on her... I need to taste her. To know she's mine.

Her lips are soft, sweet. She tastes like wine and Sadie. She gasps and I delve, my tongue finding hers.

I don't let our first kiss linger, not here on the street.

"Want more?" I ask.

She nods and licks her lips.

"Good girl." I steer her to the truck so I can get us to her place. To give us both more of what we need.

6
———

I don't know what it is about Miles that's different from other guys I dated.

No, actually, I do.

He's more attractive. More protective. More possessive. Sitting beside me in the booth, he angled his body toward me as if I were the only person he cared about. His size pretty much blocked out the restaurant and I felt like we were alone. As if I were the only thing he saw. His touches were tame, but they heated my skin. My shoulder, the line of my neck. The top of my thigh.

Then there was the way he dealt with that sleazeball

in the back hallway. I saw the anger and darkness in his gaze directed solely at the drunk guy who cornered me. But his words weren't harsh or mean. In fact, he *thanked* the guy. Of course, his tone was sarcastic and he gave him a little nudge into the wall, but he was so big and brawny in comparison that he could have beat the shit out of him if he wanted to.

I appreciated his not causing a scene or ruining our night. I'd have dwelled on it if it became a fight. Instead, he took my hand, steered me away, and kissed me.

We don't say anything on the ride to my place. Maybe it's on purpose, but maybe it's because there's some kind of heated spell cast over us. As if dinner was foreplay and the anticipation only built and made me hotter. Needier. Wetter.

When we reach my place, he takes the keys and opens the door for me. If it were any other guy, I'd think he was being a misogynistic asshole—of course I can use a set of keys!—but Miles makes me feel like he's taking care of me.

Again.

I flip the switch to light the lamp next to my sofa.

My apartment seems smaller with him in it. I swallow at the look in his eye. The heat. I remember his hands on me the night before, but it was quick and I was worried about being discovered. Dripping on his fingers because it was daring and because he was so freaking skilled.

I want more of that. Now.

"Wearing panties, sweetheart?" He shuts the front door with his foot.

I nod.

"That's good. I want that pussy covered when there's a chance another man might see it."

My mouth drops open at his possessiveness.

"Bossy much?" I arch my eyebrow.

He grunts and pushes off the door and settles himself on my sofa.

With a quick curl of his finger, he beckons me.

I follow because I want what he's offering.

He pushes the coffee table back a few inches, allowing me room to stand in front of him. He hooks a big hand around my waist and pulls me between his spread knees.

This is my apartment, and he's the one who's settled and content.

He holds out his hand, palm up. The corner of his mouth turns up as he waits.

I reach beneath my skirt, shimmy my panties down my legs, and give them to him.

"They're damp. You all wet for me, sweetheart?"

Warmth spreads across my cheeks. Of course he

points out the wetness. It's not a poke at me, but blatant proof of how virile I find him. My body craves him.

"Miles," I whisper.

"What do you need?"

"Do I... Is this one-sided?" I ask.

His eyes widen and he looks at me as if I asked if he was the Easter bunny.

He shakes his head as he undoes his belt and works open his jeans so his dick springs free. Brazenly, he strokes the swollen flesh from root to tip. It's big, like him. Thick and long. I question my ability to take him.

"I'll fit," he says, as if reading my thoughts. "You were made for me."

As he continues to stroke himself, he says, "Lift the skirt. Show me what's mine."

I lick my lips with anticipation, loving that he's taking control. That all I have to do is feel and get lost in the way he's looking at me. At the way he so blatantly wants me, too.

"This is crazy." I reach for the hem of my skirt.

"Nothing wrong with crazy." His gaze remains affixed to my fingers and the expanse of thigh that is slowly being revealed.

"I'm a detective investigating you," I remind him.

We didn't talk about my work at all through dinner. Only a little on the drive.

"You know I'm innocent, otherwise you wouldn't be showing me—*fuck*, baby—that pretty little pussy."

My skirt is crumpled in my grip and he can see all of me from the waist down. Bare for him.

His blue eyes meet mine as his hand stills around his dick.

"You want to stop? You want me to leave so you can get the proof you need that backs my words and your instinct? You want to delay what's going to happen between us just because your partner might get a little pissy?"

I shake my head.

"Good. I don't want to talk about Peterson or this investigation while my dick's out and your slit is shining for me. You know his thoughts are flawed."

"Miles," I whisper.

"You decide, sweetheart. I'll go with whatever you decide. I'll only touch you if you're with me one hundred percent."

Am I crazy? Yes. Am I stupid? No. I won't lose my job over this because there's no evidence of Miles being involved in the murder in any way. Sure, I could make for a terrible witness on the stand if it ever got to that. But it won't. It *can't* because Miles wasn't involved.

"Okay."

"Okay, what?"

"Okay, I'm all in."

A smile curls his lips and he looks almost feral. "Be a good girl and turn around. Bend over and put your hands on the coffee table, ass up, so I can eat that pussy for dessert."

Oh. My. God.

He waits, one hand around his dick, one on his thick thigh.

I turn, stare at the hall to my bedroom, and then lean forward.

He grips my hips, and I gasp as he pulls me back. At the first lick of his tongue, I cry out and arch my back.

"Fuck, yes." He fans my sensitive flesh.

Then he gets to work *eating* me. Not one part of my pussy is neglected. I drop my head and I can see between my parted legs his dick—its hunger and thickness as it protrudes from the front of his jeans and boxers, as if it can't be contained. There's a pearly drop of fluid at the slit and I want to taste him as he's tasting me.

Except I'm not moving anywhere. He's got me in a secure hold and his mouth is on me. Latched on, sucking and licking my clit as if I'm his first meal after he's been rescued from a deserted island.

"Miles!" I cry out.

"That's it. Ride my face."

I'm shameless. Wanton. Completely uninhibited as he brings me to the brink of orgasm, and then over.

I come on a moan.

He turns me easily since I'm replete and wobbly-legged. His mouth glistens and he uses the back of his hand to wipe it. It's so hot, my pussy clenches even though I just came.

He reaches for his wallet, pulls out a condom and rolls it on with deft fingers. An easy tug and I drop onto the couch with him, straddling his waist.

A big hand cups the back of my neck as he kisses me. I taste myself on his tongue and I love it. I've had lovers before, but it wasn't like this. So carnal. So...*raw*.

I want more ,and by the way his jaw is tight, his muscles tense, and his dick even thicker and longer than before, I can tell he's holding himself back.

I don't want that. I want all of Miles. His wildness. His intensity.

Lifting up on my knees, I hover over him. He shifts, pushing his jeans down and out of the way. I close my eyes and lower myself.

"Don't close them," he says.

I open my eyes and gaze at him as I take him into my body, one delicious, thick inch at a time.

"Fuck," he growls, gripping me my hips.

He's big, and a tight fit. I'm so wet though that he slips in easily, filling me.

When I'm sitting on his thighs, taking all of him, his head falls back against the couch.

"Fuck."

I start to move and he shakes his head. Reaching up, he lifts my shirt and rids me of it with one yank. My bra falls away with expert precision. Only my skirt remains, bunched about my waist.

"Better. Now ride me, sweetheart."

I do. We get lost in each other, my orgasm building ridiculously fast since I already came once.

"Shit, I'm going to come. Too fast," he admits. "You're too perfect."

He licks his thumb and reaches between us, working my clit in small circles. It doesn't take long, and I come around him, my inner muscles clenching hard, which sets him off too.

The tight clutch of his fingers on my hips keeps me in place as he buries himself deep and lets go.

We're sweaty and satisfied. Breathless and boneless.

He kisses my temple. "I'm not done with you."

I gasp when he stands, keeping me in his arms. I wrap my legs around his waist to cling to him.

"That's round one." He carries me down the hall to my bed. "It's going to be a long night."

7

———

$\mathcal{M}$ILES

I WAKE to the sun streaming through the window, and—

"Oh, fuck," I say out loud.

I didn't mean to spend the night. What the hell time is it, anyway? I scramble out of bed to find my jeans. My phone is in my jeans, right?

"Hey, Sadie—" I look down at the rumpled bed.

No Sadie.

Did I truly just get out of her bed and not realize she wasn't in it? Of course she's not here. She probably had to get up and go to work. I don't even know what day it is.

Two weeks in Montana and I've lost all concept of time. Every day is a workday on the ranch.

I find my jeans slung over her closet door and grab the phone out of the pocket. It's nearly dead. Fuck it all. It's nine thirty. I have about ten texts, all of which I ignore.

Chance makes a big fucking deal out of starting each morning at six. He's determined—or our esteemed father is determined from the grave—that we'll learn to do everything on the damned ranch, or we won't get our billion.

Whatever. If Chance ever gets a woman into bed, I sure as hell hope he sleeps in.

I hastily pull the jeans over my legs and hips and walk out of Sadie's bedroom.

"Hey, sleepyhead." She smiles and then takes a sip out of a mug. "Coffee?"

I stop, surprised. "Don't you have to work?" I scratch my head.

"Not on Saturday, silly." She smiles at me, her hair a mess, but in a *recently fucked* way.

"Is it Saturday?"

She laughs. "Uh...yeah. You seriously don't know what day it is?"

I frown. "Hell, no. Chance has Austin and me working around the clock at that damned ranch. I'll be in the doghouse for sure for not showing up for breakfast at six this morning."

Not that I care. No way would I turn down waking at dawn to Sadie beneath the covers and my dick in her mouth for anything.

"He keeps you on a short leash."

"He can also fuck himself," I mutter.

She rises, pads to the coffee maker on the counter, and pours another cup. "Cream and sugar?"

"Hell no," I practically growl.

"You got it." She hands me the mug and our fingers brush against each other.

And damn if I don't feel that tiny touch in my cock. It jerks against the denim of my jeans as I remember all the different ways I had her during the night. I'm pretty sure we might have been upside down at one point.

Sadie looks like a dream in a short red satin robe. I could easily brush it off her shoulders, spread those luscious legs, and bring her to a couple more climaxes right here in her little kitchen. On her table, spread out like a feast. I lick my lips, and not for coffee.

"So it's Saturday," I say, noticing how her nipples are outlined through the thin fabric.

"All day," she replies.

"Okay. That means we met on a Thursday evening."

"Right again."

"Why was your friend Stacy—"

"Tracy."

I take a sip of coffee. Damn, I want Sadie again, but it probably won't happen. She has to be sore. "Sorry, why was *Tracy* having a bachelorette party on a Thursday evening? Isn't that usually a weekend thing?"

She shrugs and her robe slips a little, baring slightly more of her milky shoulder. "Not when the bride works every weekend. She's a cocktail waitress at the same bar where the party was, and Friday, Saturday, and Sunday are her biggest nights for tips."

"Ah. Got it."

In fact...

I jolt at a knock on her door. Who the hell is getting in the way of me being with my woman? She cocks her head at me and gives me a look I can't read.

"What?" I ask.

"Do you mind?" She cocks her hip.

"Do I mind what?"

"Going into the bedroom? I have no idea who that is."

I sure as hell do fucking mind. I know sleeping with a detective who's working on a murder investigation in which I'm a primary suspect isn't the best idea, but I have nothing to hide. Of course it could be her mother or something. Except doesn't her mother do hair in Billings? Besides, I'm not going to get into a relationship where my woman is afraid to let anyone know we're together.

Fuck. Are we even together? Didn't I tell her I don't do relationships?

I did. But I also said I want more of her. That her pussy was mine. And I reinforced that every time I filled her with my dick and made her come all over it. And that happened a hell of a lot last night. On her couch and in her bed.

"No fucking way you're answering the door to anyone dressed like that." I pointedly take in the skimpy robe as I cross my arms.

She frowns, but when I stay quiet and continue to glare, she storms past me into her bedroom. Over my shoulder, I watch her fling off the robe and tug on sweats and a hoodie sweatshirt.

She's naked underneath, but the thick cotton hides it all from neck to ankle.

Much better. I nod and she sighs, gives me an eye roll, and pulls the bedroom door shut behind her. Me on one side, her front door on the other.

I take another sip of coffee. Damn it to hell. The woman makes good strong coffee too. Is there anything she can't do?

Judging by last night and her rumpled bedding, I'd say the answer's no.

But judging by this morning, she's not fully on board yet. But I am. I plan to spend more than one night with her.

Except she can't let anyone know I'm here. I'll respect that, for now. It doesn't mean I have to like it. Besides, who the hell is at her door on a Saturday morning, anyway?

I quickly dress and take a look at my texts while I wait. A couple from Chance wondering where I am and when I'm going to get back do my share of the fucking work.

The saying is bros before hoes, but Sadie's not a hoe. I bet Austin slept in with Carly in his bed. Chance is just cranky because he's the only one not getting any.

I ignore the texts...and him.

I scroll on. Two spam messages. Another from a woman named Rhonda.

Rhonda...

Right. She's a woman I hooked up with before I came to Montana. Bleached blond and big-breasted. Not usually my type, but I was horny and she was there. That was before I knew Sadie even existed. Now, thinking of Rhonda, my dick doesn't even twitch.

What does she do for a living? Hell, I can't remember. Nails, maybe? More importantly, how the fuck did she get my number?

I read the text again.

Hey, Miles. It's Rhonda Grimes. We got together a while back. Could you call me? It's important.

Not as important as gorgeous Sadie in the other room.

Gorgeous Sadie who doesn't want anyone to know I'm here.

Fuck this garbage. I just watched Austin have to tiptoe around Carly's father. I'm not doing the same thing. I respect Sadie, but I'm fully dressed and there's no reason why I can't show myself.

I run my hand through my hair and walk out of the bedroom.

Sadie gasps and I glare at the visitor. Thank God she changed.

"Bridger," Mark Peterson says. "What the hell is he doing here, Sadie?"

8

SADIE

I'M glad Miles insisted I change. I hate the way Mark ogles me when I'm fully dressed. Having him see me in my silky robe would have made me feel gross. Still, in my thick sweats, I cross my arms over my chest. I'm not wearing a bra and there's no way I'm letting Mark figure that out.

"He... He just dropped by to bring me some information on the case," I say quickly.

"Oh? You've got new information, Bridger?" Mark eyes Miles, who is fully dressed, thank God. "Why didn't you call me? I'm the lead on this case, not my partner here.

Besides, didn't you swear to God and back that you and your other brother had nothing to do with anything?"

Shit. I've just made things worse for Miles.

And for myself.

But damn him, anyway. He could've stayed in the bedroom.

Miles is staring at me. I can't look him in the eye, but I feel it—that fiery glare that's probably a sign I'm going to get a spanking or something later. Why that appeals to me, I have no idea.

"Turned out to be nothing," Miles says.

"I'll be the judge of that." Mark stalks toward Miles but stops, leaving about ten feet between them.

Good call.

Miles does *not* look happy.

I don't blame him. But what did he expect me to do? I'm investigating a case, and he's a...

Well, Mark would say he's a suspect. I disagree with that assessment. But no matter the evidence, he's a person of interest along with both his brothers. If Mark knows I'm sleeping with Miles, he'll take me off the case. Or worse, have me fired.

Only Sheriff Bryant or Mayor Vance can technically fire me, but Mark's got a lot of seniority. It would be more to use against Miles, spinning it so it looked as if Miles slept with me to mess with the case instead of what it really was. Which was... I have no idea.

Fuck! I knew I shouldn't have accepted Miles's dinner invitation. I knew it, but I did it anyway.

I did it because I like him.

I more than like him. He's amazing. He had me feeling things last night that I've never felt. I don't just mean ridiculously amazing orgasms either. I like *him* and how he makes me feel.

Miles towers over Mark, but I'll give Mark a gold star for meeting Miles's gaze. It's more than I can do at the moment.

"So what is it, Bridger?" he asks.

"Like I said," Miles says through clenched teeth, "it turned out to be nothing."

"And like *I* said. I'll be the judge."

Time for me to intervene. "I already exercised judgment. It's irrelevant."

"What was it, Bridger?" Mark pushes.

"Jesus. The answer's still the same. Nothing." Miles brushes past Mark briskly and stands by the door.

"Wait a minute," Mark yells at him.

"Let him go." I set my hand on Mark's arm to hold him back. "It was nothing."

Mark rakes his gaze over my body and I snatch my hand back.

"Just what the hell is going on here, Hopkins?"

"Nothing that's any of your business."

He narrows his eyes. "It sure as hell is my business if Bridger is keeping evidence from me."

I rub my forehead, trying to ease the ache that has erupted. "It's nothing. I lied. He was here because I invited him."

He's quiet for a moment. Too long. I keep myself from squirming in the chair.

Finally—

"I see."

"For breakfast. Just for breakfast."

"And you met him in that?" He points to grungy sweats.

For God's sake, Sadie. Grow a spine!

"We had dinner last night. He stayed over. Are you satisfied?"

The tension in my living room could be cut with a knife. I'm not ashamed I was with Miles. It was amazing. I also don't want Mark to know about my sex life. Ever. It isn't his business and it gives me the creeps.

But I crossed a line.

"I knew I saw a glimmer of recognition in his eye yesterday when we were at their house." He spins at Miles and points.

"I'm a grown woman, Mark," I reply. "Who I see on my off-time is my own business."

"Not when it's a suspect in a case you're investigating!"

Miles pushes past Mark and stands in front of me, blocking the guy from getting to me. "You don't talk to her like that."

I like how he's protecting me, but I did this to myself. Of course, he could have stayed in the bedroom, but that wouldn't have been fair either.

"For the last damned time, the Bridger brothers are *not* suspects." I step around Miles's big frame. "I don't care what kind of beef you have with their old man. They're not him."

Mark rolls his shoulders back. Points at me this time. "You're off this case, Hopkins."

I sigh, knowing I just fucked up my career. "Fine. Whatever."

"I ought to go to the sheriff about this." Mark sounds petty. Like a high schooler.

"Go ahead."

"But I won't."

God, here it comes. He's going to want something in return. A blowjob? Or something even more disgusting? Not that he'd tell me his expectations in front of Miles.

"All right. Thank you." It's easier to placate the man than argue.

"You're a good cop, Sadie. I don't want to take you off the case."

"Then don't."

"Are you willing to forget about him?" Mark gestures to Miles.

I look at the guy who's only been nice to me. Kind. Attentive. Thorough.

No.

The word is lodged in the back of my throat, and it desperately wants out.

But I also love my work, and this dead body is the most exciting case to come out of Bayfield in the little over a year that I've been here.

"Mark," I say. "Who I see is my own business. If evidence comes to light linking Miles to the body, I will stop seeing him or I will recuse myself from the case. But until then, there's no reason for me not to see him."

A giant cement block lifts from my shoulders.

I stood up for myself. I stood up for Miles.

It feels damned good. What's happening between us is real.

Why didn't I just do that in the first place instead of telling Mark that Miles had come over to talk to me about the case? Instead, I made what we did seem naughty or illicit. We are grown-ups on our own time doing our own thing.

I offer a glance up at Miles, whose jaw is clenched, and he's glaring daggers at Mark. His anger is directed at my partner right now, but I'm sure some of it is for me. That I asked him to hide in the bedroom in the first place. He probably thinks I feel it was tawdry and wrong.

It doesn't feel wrong. It feels...right.

God, one night and I'm in trouble. I ache for him to tell me I'm his good girl once more. To look at me as he did last night. Even a short time ago.

He has to forgive me. He has to. I don't want to give him up.

"Have it your way, Hopkins. I think you're headed for heartache." He nods to the files he brought over. "Analyze those. I want a full report Monday morning."

Not only do I have to work all weekend, I probably won't see Miles again once he walks out that door.

I think you're headed for heartache.

Mark was wrong. I'm already there.

9

———————

$\mathcal{M}$ILES

"Miles…"

Damn her. Damn Sadie Hopkins. I brush past her to the door, even though every cell in my body is screaming to stay. To throw her over my shoulder and take her back to bed. To fuck her hard. To spank that creamy white ass for lying about us.

Sure, she eventually told the truth, but still…

"Don't go," she pleads.

God, that voice. That sweet and tender voice—the voice that called my name so many times last night.

She has the voice of an angel, and the growling moans of a little devil.

And I adore both sides of her.

Except the side that's ashamed of what we've done.

"I have to go," I say without turning around.

But then her touch...

First on my shoulder, and then on my hips. Then her front melting against my back. She's so much smaller than I am. Her forehead is between my shoulder blades, her breasts against my back.

But no.

I thought she was mine, but she's not. Sure, she stood up for us when pushed, but her first inclination was to lie. This is why I don't do relationships. They suck. I always get fucked over in the end because I always end up the last priority. I turn around and detach her from me.

"You made your feelings clear," I tell her.

"Yeah, I did. I told him the truth."

I scoff. "It doesn't count when you lie first. If you don't put value on what we have. Or more accurately, what we *could* have."

My mother didn't put value on her relationships. Or on me. Jonathan Bridger was the first of many men. Instead of getting a huge cash payout from him, she got me. But she learned from the experience—to get better birth control, for sure—and moved on to her next conquest. And then the next. I have no idea which husband she's on. I've lost count. It's her job—marrying and then divorcing and taking half.

I learned from my mother what I didn't want in a relationship. A gold digger, for sure. That's not what Sadie is. She didn't know who I was any more than I knew she was a detective in the bar the other night. But I don't commit. Ever. Because I don't trust.

I let Sadie in last night more than any other woman. I thought what we shared, what we had, was real. Was *more*.

Then she went and devalued it with Peterson. Kept doing it by placing me last, not first.

The case came first for her.

She blinks and wipes her palms on her sweats. "I... I panicked, okay? Have you never panicked in your life?"

I cross my arms over my chest. "Not over spending the night with anyone."

"Because they were flings and didn't mean anything to you. Right?"

I can't argue about that. I don't do relationships, but I was willing to give it a go with Sadie. It's better to know now where I stand. "So you're saying this isn't a fling and it means something. And yet you lied to Mark."

"He's my boss!" she all but shouts. "This case..."

I shake my head, ready to make a few points, when my

phone dings again with a text. Damn, it was nearly dead an hour ago. How is it still hanging on?

I grab it out of my pocket.

Chance. Again.

I ignore it.

I'll be home shortly, and I'm looking forward to one of his days of hard labor. I'll need it to work off the tension I'm feeling. The anger. Damn, I'm pissed. I'm pissed at this gorgeous woman who I thought might be different.

In the end, they're all shallow. Lesson learned. I won't be fooled twice.

"Please, Miles."

"I have to go."

"Will you call me?"

I don't turn to meet her gaze. I don't because I know if I do, I'll forgive her, grab her, kiss her senseless. She doesn't know about my past, that my role model for relationships is shit. I just expected her to be all in. Or at least all in about me.

I can't give her an answer. Not until I've had a chance to think about everything.

So I leave.

I leave, and I close the door behind me.

———

I DON'T OFFER any explanation to Chance or Austin about where I was, and they don't ask, which surprises me. After a day of muscle-grinding work—loading hay bales into a loft is hard as fuck—I shower and meet my brothers out on the deck for a well-earned cold one.

I want to go for a ride and clear my head, but a storm's coming in, the clouds moving fast from the west.

Carly joins us and Austin tugs her onto his lap. She's drinking diet soda instead of beer.

"Don't like beer, Carly?" I ask.

She shrugs and settles into Austin's hold. "It's okay. I just don't feel like one."

"So...do you live here now?"

Sure, I'm being blunt, but that's me.

"You got a problem with that?" Austin eyes me.

I take a long drink of the cold brew and then I shake my head. "Nope. Sorry. I didn't mean that the way it sounded. Of course you're welcome here."

She smiles. "I know that. Are you okay?"

I draw in a breath. What a fucking loaded question. I take another sip. Then, "Yeah. Fine."

"Don't pull that shit," Austin says, after a swallow. "We haven't been brothers for long, but I can tell when something's bothering you."

"I'm guessing it has something to do with where he spent the night." From Chance.

"Leave him alone," Carly says. "It's none of your business. You both sound like my dad."

That gets a laugh out of Austin and a chuckle out of Chance.

"I will be moving in," Carly continues. "Austin and I have discussed it, and though my parents aren't thrilled, they finally accept that I'm an adult and it's my decision."

"I'll be putting a ring on that finger before long." Austin takes her hand and rubs his fingers into her palm. "Soon as I get my billions."

"Billion," Chance says. "You get a billion. Singular."

"Only a billion?" I roll my eyes and take another drink of beer. "How *will* we survive?" I hold up my empty bottle. "Chance, bring out that MacAllan. I need something a little stronger."

"After dinner," Chance says.

"No." I'm in no mood to be told no tonight, especially not by my tank of a little brother. "I want some now."

"That means something's wrong. What's up?" Austin demands. "This isn't you talking, Miles. Chance is the grump."

"Hey!" Chance counters.

Austin ignores him and keeps going. "I'm the guy who goes off halfcocked and you're the brooder. And you're brooding a hell of a lot more than usual."

I look at him and glare. Brooding. "How the fuck would you know? You don't know anything about me."

Except I *am* a fucking brooder.

"No biggie." Chance rises. "I'll get the scotch. But Louisa'll have dinner ready in half an hour or so."

Half an hour? In a half hour I'm planning to be drunk off my ass.

Damn. I thought a day of grinding work would ease the tension out of my bones, but it didn't. I'm still just as pissed off.

And I still fucking miss her.

I miss Sadie Hopkins. The woman I barely know but can't get out of my head.

Fuck her, anyway.

"Miles," Carly says, "what's the matter?"

"I'm fine," I say a little more harshly than I mean to.

"Dude"—Austin eyeballs me—"don't take your bad mood out on my woman. It's not fair."

He's right, of course. "Sorry," I mumble, slumping lower in the chair.

"Can we do anything to help?" Carly asks.

"I wish you could." I turn to my brother. "Be good to her, man. She's a keeper."

"I plan on it." Austin finishes the last of his beer and sets the bottle down on the deck railing. "What's eating you, Miles?"

If I could only put it into words. But nothing makes sense. I don't do relationships, so why am I tangled up in knots over a woman who clearly doesn't want to be with me? A woman who lied about being with me? Sure, she eventually came clean, but still... Should I cut her a little more slack? She *is* a detective on a case involving my family.

God, if only she didn't feel like the most perfect glove around my cock...

"Where the hell is Chance with that scotch?" I glance toward the French doors leading into the house.

"Right here." Chance comes out and sets the bottle and a lowball glass in front of me. "Help yourself."

"Aren't any of you going to join me?"

"Happy to," Chance says. "After dinner."

"For Christ's sake." I open the bottle, pour myself two fingers of the amber liquid, and take a taste, letting the warmth and smokiness settle over my tongue before it trickles down my throat.

I'm not a big drinker. Hell, drinking doesn't solve anything. I set the glass on the table. "Sorry, Chance," I mutter. "Sorry to all of you. I'm being an asshole."

"When you're right, you're right." Chance glances at my drink. "I know we're billionaires and all—eventually, anyway—but my ma taught me never to waste anything."

"I'll drink it. But you're right. It's more of an after-dinner drink, especially after a hard day's work."

"You want another cold one?" Austin asks.

"No, but thanks. I'll be fine. I always am."

Austin opens his mouth to reply, but before he can, Louisa opens the French doors.

"Looks like dinner's on," Chance says.

"Not quite yet," Louisa says. "It'll be another fifteen minutes. But there's someone at the door to see Miles."

I widen my eyes. "Who is it?"

"The detective from yesterday," she says.

Fuck. Peterson.

"That man can't leave us alone," Chance mutters.

Could this day get any worse? I pick up the scotch. I'll be needing it after all.

10

MILES APPROACHES, holding a cocktail. Looks like bourbon or scotch.

He rakes his gaze over me, stopping at the black skirt —the one I wore the night before.

He looks so good. I want to go to him, go up on my tiptoes and kiss him, feel the rasp of his late-day whiskers against my lips. He's in jeans and a T-shirt, both dusty. His hair's a mess and it looks like he spent a hard day working the ranch.

"*Detective Hopkins.*" His voice is deep and rumbly. "I thought it would be Peterson at the door."

"Why would you think that?"

"Because our housekeeper said the detective from yesterday wanted to see me. I just assumed…"

"If you think Mark Peterson will go anywhere on a Saturday evening that isn't the pool hall, you don't know him very well."

"He came to your house this morning," Miles reminds me.

"That was for me to do his work for him," I mutter.

"I know him as well as I care to." He looks away from me. "What do you want, Detective?"

I chew on my lower lip and inhale. His scent rushes into me—all woods and spice and man. "I'm so sorry, Miles. About this morning. I made a complete mess of everything."

He crosses his arms over his chest, just as he did this morning. His biceps bulge, and I remember how solid every inch of him is. He meets my gaze.

"You'll get no argument from me."

I bite my lip. "How can I make this right?"

"Wearing that skirt's a nice touch, but you fucked up, Sadie."

I nod earnestly. "I know. I'm so pissed at myself. But you heard me. I leveled with Mark."

"Eventually."

"Yeah…eventually. I don't have a billion dollars coming my way. I need my job."

"Don't toss the will in my face."

"Fine, but I *do* need my job. You know it's not a good thing for a detective to be in a relationship with a suspect. I know you're not one. I told you that and you know I told Mark that. But *he* thinks you are and he's my boss."

I glance down at the glossy hardwood floor at my feet. "I don't know what this is between us, but I like it. It's… different. While I feel like I've known you forever, I haven't. And you don't know me."

He's quiet—too quiet—so I push on.

"Aren't I entitled to one mistake? Are you going to tell me you've never fucked anything up?"

He still doesn't reply.

Moments pass, and just as I'm about to give up, Chance Bridger walks toward us.

"Hey, Sadie. What are you doing here?"

"I just came to talk to Miles."

"Update on the case? Serving a warrant?"

I shake my head. "No. Nothing like that."

I don't elaborate. It's one thing for me to come clean with Mark when he caught me and Miles together. It's another with Miles's brother. I don't know what Miles has shared about us and I don't want to mess things up further.

"Well, dinner's ready. You want to join us? Louisa makes enough to feed an army. We always have leftovers."

I glance at Miles. His expression is noncommittal. I don't want to leave. I want to stay and have Miles accept my apology.

"Uh...yeah, okay. That'd be nice."

"Come on in. We eat in the kitchen."

I'm not sure why Chance is being so nice. He wasn't thrilled when Mark and I showed up yesterday morning. None of them let us in the house. While I wasn't going to go snooping, they were right about Mark. He would have taken the opportunity to ferret out any kind of weakness or sign of guilt he found.

From what I could tell—although I didn't take any real time to look around—the house wasn't going to have a smoking gun or a blood-covered rock or some other kind of murder weapon lying around.

I have to assume Chance's dislike is for Mark alone. Whatever the reason, I'm thankful he's given me the opportunity to stay.

I follow Chance, and I assume Miles follows me. I don't dare look over my shoulder.

"You know Austin," Chance says, "and this is his girl-friend, Carly Vance. Carly, Sadie Hopkins."

"Hi, Sadie." Carly smiles.

I've seen her before, and then it clicks. "Vance. You're the mayor's daughter."

She nods. "I am, but I work here as a vet tech." She lifts her gaze to Austin. "And this big guy is mine."

Ah, the girlfriend. They look sweet together, and in love. That was fast. Austin has only been in town as long as Miles.

"Won't you sit down?" She pats the chair next to her.

Perfect. An ally. Maybe. Someone who understands falling for a Bridger man happens fast.

Everyone else sits around the table, including Miles after he washed his hands at the sink. He settles into the empty seat next to me.

"And this is our housekeeper, Louisa," Chance says. "She's an amazing cook and keeps us from withering away."

I glance up at the older woman who's carrying in a large serving dish, her hands covered in oven mitts. "Nice to meet you, Louisa."

She offers me a smile as she places the dish on a trivet. "You too, Sadie. I hope you like lasagna."

"I love it." I inhale. "It smells terrific."

"What can I get you to drink?" Louisa asks.

I gaze around the table. Austin and Chance are drinking beer, and Carly is drinking water. I need to keep my wits about me if I'm going to get Miles back on my side. And back into my bed.

"Just water, please."

"Absolutely."

A moment later, Louisa slides a glass of water in front of me, and Carly passes me the salad bowl. I help myself to a modest portion and then hand the bowl to Miles beside me. He takes it.

Is that a good sign?

I guess we'll see.

Miles downs the brown liquid in the glass he's been holding since I arrived and then takes a drink from his glass of water.

"So what brings you here on a Saturday, Sadie?" Chance asks.

I hastily finish chewing my bite of salad and swallow. "I came to see Miles."

"How'd he get so lucky?" Austin asks.

My cheeks burn, then, and the table gets quiet.

Do they know?

Miles rises and sets his napkin on the table. "Excuse me for a minute."

Then all eyes are on me. Austin's dark ones. Chance's baby blues. Carly's, which are a gorgeous green. Even Louisa's.

None of us can miss an exterior door slamming shut.

"I..."

"It's okay." Carly pats my forearm. "You don't have to say anything."

"Miles is a good guy," Austin says. "This just all gets to us from time to time. The whole will thing. While I have Carly here, it's hard to be forced to stay at this place for a year. My mom's sick and in Seattle." He runs a hand through his hair. "Now the dead body surfacing after we cleaned up that dam. It's a lot to process."

I nod. "Of course. I understand."

"Something's bothering him," Carly says. "Do you know what it might be?"

"I have an idea," I say.

"What can we do to help?"

"I don't think there's anything you can do." I rise. "I'll take care of it. Where did he go?"

"Probably to the garage to work on that bike of his," Chance says and rises. "Sit down, Sadie. I'll get him."

I shake my head. "It's okay. This is all my fault."

"How is it your fault?" Austin asks.

Carly pokes him. "Mind your business."

Austin widens his eyes, obviously just catching on. "Oh."

Okay, so they don't know. Correction—they *didn't* know. They do now. Clearly Miles didn't mention "us" to his family. Can't say I blame him, after I couldn't bring myself to tell Mark the truth at first.

If he's not interested in more, telling his brothers about one amazing night with me wasn't necessary. Or maybe he doesn't kiss and tell, which is good, but his abrupt departure from the table means he's still pissed. Either way, I'm in big trouble.

I plunk back down into my seat, feeling defeated. "Tell me how to fix this."

"We don't know our brother that well yet, Sadie," Chance says. "But you *are* a detective on a case that involves our land. Us."

"Yeah. But I don't for a minute think any of you were involved. He knows that."

"Your partner seems to think otherwise." Chance clenches his jaw.

I frown. "He's trying to be a hard-ass, but he'll see reason. He's a good cop...for the most part."

"For the most part?" Austin raises his eyebrows.

"He goes a little...*vigilante* sometimes. I mean, it's pretty slow around this cow town most of the time, so he's gunning to make an arrest and solve this dead body case. It's not too often we have one, so it's a big deal. But he'll see reason, and the evidence. And if he doesn't, I'll go over his head if I have to."

"To the sheriff?" Austin asks.

I shrug. "Yeah. Or to the mayor. I hate to do it, but the evidence doesn't support any of you being involved."

"Thanks." Chance leans back in his chair. "That means a lot to us. And I promise you that we—my brothers and I—had nothing to do with that poor soul who lost his life somewhere on this ranch. My dad had a lot of enemies. Apparently a lot more than I even knew about."

"The guy was a dick." Austin shakes his head. "He knocked up my mother and then left when she found out she was pregnant. He did the same to Miles's mom. And then he divorced Chance's eventually as well. We never met or talked to each other until a few weeks ago."

"Yeah, I've heard the story. I'm sorry you all didn't get to grow up together."

"We know about each other now," Chance says. "It was tough going at first, but we're mellowing."

Austin huffs out a laugh. Apparently *tough* has a story or two behind it.

"Can you tell me about Miles? About how he grew up?"

Chance shakes his head. "We've met Austin's mom, but Miles hasn't shared any of his own details with us."

Hmmm. That's interesting. What secrets is Miles Bridger hiding, if any? And are they why he was so quick to react?

I will find out. I rise again. "I'm going to find him."

Austin points across the kitchen. "Go out the back door off the kitchen and try the detached garage outside, the first one."

"Okay. Thanks for dinner. Well, for the bite of salad, anyway."

"It'll still be here," Carly says. "Good luck."

I smile at her. "Thanks."

I've a feeling I'm going to need it.

11

———

Miles

"Fuck!" I curse at my phone's ringtone. I don't recognize the number.

I'm pacing in front of my motorcycle and take in the dented chrome, the torn seat. Faded paint job. The scent of motor oil is like a familiar balm. I can't wait to get my hands on my latest project. I'll work a few hours on her later, starting to take her apart to fix her up. It'll ease this...aggravation.

No. *Anger.*

At who, though?

I put the phone to my ear when it rings again. "What is it?" I snarl.

I'm frustrated with myself. With Sadie.

"Hello...Miles? Miles Bridger?" A woman.

"Yeah, who's asking?"

"This is Rhonda. We...you know...hooked up a while back?"

Right. Rhonda. The text earlier.

"Sure. What's up?"

"Did you get my message from yesterday?'

Shit, yeah. "I did. I've been busy. What do you need?"

She clears her throat, a crackle through the phone line. "I've been trying to get in touch with you for a week. I finally got someone from your shop to give me your cell number."

"Oh? Who?"

"I think his name was Dave."

Dave Wilson, one of my mechanics in New York. He's fired. This is my private number, not something *anyone* shares.

"What can I help you with, Rhonda?"

"Well, I—"

The door hinges squeak. Sadie steps into the garage and looks around, her gaze stopping on me.

In that damned black skirt, her bare legs going from here to heaven. Fuck!

"I have to call you back," I say to Rhonda, ending the call.

Sadie takes a tentative step toward me. Then another. I don't say anything as she makes her approach.

She tips her chin up when she's right before me. "You're being an asshole."

I lift my eyebrows. Her words are completely unexpected.

"Me? I'm not the one who's ashamed of us."

"Have you told your brothers about us?"

Well, shit.

She shifts her hands to her hips.

"No."

"Why's that?" She tilts her head.

"It's none of their business."

"Just like it's none of Mark's business," she counters.

Fuck, she has a point.

"Are you going to get fired and lose your income if Austin and Chance have an issue with us being together, even though you know I've already told them I don't think any of you had anything to do with the murder?"

I open my mouth. Close it.

"Just as I thought." She spins around, walks away, and then looks over her shoulder. "Let me know when you get your head out of your ass." Those words are tossed over her shoulder.

Fuck. Me.

"Wait."

She stills but doesn't turn.

"You're right. I am an asshole." I approach her slowly. With the same caution as one would take when trying to touch a wildcat, I put my hands on Sadie's hips, lean down, and kiss her shoulder.

She turns in the circle of my arms. "What set you off?"

I reach up and stroke her sleek hair. "My mother changes men at the same pace most people change their sheets. She's a shitty example of being in a solid relationship. So I don't do them. I've been with women, but they know the score. One and done."

"I wasn't asking for a ring, Miles."

I shake my head. "This is different. Hell, I have no idea what it is about you that drives me fucking nuts. That makes me want to sink myself balls deep in you and stay there forever."

Her cheeks flush at my bold words.

I sigh. "When you didn't tell Peterson about us, I figured it didn't mean anything. That *we* didn't. That your feelings didn't match mine."

She drops her gaze to my chest and settles a hand over my heart. "I don't *know* how you're feeling."

"I thought I made myself pretty clear. At the restaurant. At your apartment."

She shakes her head.

"Fine." I tip her chin up with my fingers. "I want more with you, Sadie. I want to see where this goes. I'm into you. Into trying for an 'us.'"

She blinks and a smile turns up the corner of her mouth. "Okay."

I can't help but smile in return. "Okay?"

"Okay. Mark knows about us. He says he won't tell anyone, but I can't say he will make it easy for me."

I frown. Thinking about the annoying fucker makes my muscles twitch. "I can handle him."

"I can't lose my job," she says. "While I don't think it's fair, the fact that we even *like* each other makes it a possibility—"

"We *like* each other?" I let a smirk spread across my face.

"But this case could be in jeopardy if I ever have to testify. It's not about you and me. It's about the law. I don't want someone to go free solely because of a conflict of interest."

"I get it."

"I'm not your mom or any of the other women you've been with."

I look her over, remembering what every dip and curve of her body looks like. Tastes like.

"I'm well aware of that."

"Then don't treat me like them."

I nod, and then I lower my head to brush my lips across hers.

They're soft and perfect, just as I remember.

My cell chimes in my pocket. A text.

I sigh, pull it out. Read the screen.

This is Rhonda. You hung up on me, so I'm texting. I'm pregnant. The baby's yours.

"What the fuck?" I rake my fingers through my hair, my entire body going numb.

Sadie grabs my wrist to look at my phone.

She steps back, her eyes wide, and all heat from just a few seconds ago is gone.

"Yeah, Miles. What the fuck?"

12

Sadie

THIS IS RHONDA. You hung up on me, so I'm texting. I'm pregnant. The baby's yours.

Already I've committed the text to memory. The words pound into my brain in synchrony with my heartbeat.

This can't be happening, especially after the fight we just had.

"This is bullshit." Miles paces the room. I've seen him angry before, but this is a whole new level. "We used protection."

"Yeah?" I whip my hands to my hips. I don't like hearing about the guy I'm into talking about sleeping with another woman. And impregnating her. "Let me guess. *'Don't worry, baby. I'm on the pill. I've got it covered.'*"

Miles stops and meets my gaze, his blue eyes on fire. "I don't go out in a storm without a raincoat. Ever."

Nice.

"Raincoats sometimes have holes in them," I counter. We used condoms last night, thank God.

"Jesus Fuck! That's not the same and you know it."

"Do I?"

He rakes his hand through his hair, holding it back for a moment. "I hardly remember her, Sadie."

Just what I want to hear.

"Great. That makes me feel a lot better. You liked her enough to fuck her but not enough to remember her. Plus, if you can't remember the woman, how can you be sure you put on a condom?"

His gaze narrows. "Because I *always* put on a goddamned condom! I put one on with you, didn't I?"

Damn. I feel like someone just lodged a bullet right in the middle of my heart. Didn't he just say I was different? That he was feeling something more? But now I'm in the same category as Rhonda, whoever the hell she is. Just some woman he put a condom on for because that's what he always does. He needs that thin latex barrier not only as protection from an STD and a baby, but from getting too close to a woman.

I hold back a sniffle. No way is Miles Bridger going to bring me to tears. I won't give him that power.

"If I'm *just* another woman, then I'm out of here." I turn again but I don't move.

Not yet.

Because he's going to stop me, like he did last time. Isn't he?

"Sadie," he groans, but doesn't come over.

I count to five and then I walk forward, to the door, and out of the garage. I can't stand the pungent smell of motor oil anyway. And Miles Bridger? He's just another dick on the long list of dicks I've fallen for.

Who needs this? Who needs whiplash being with a guy like him? I count myself lucky I didn't get in any deeper with him. One minute he's pissed at me for supposedly being ashamed of what's between us. The next, he's got a baby on the way. With someone else.

Sure, I never took Miles for a virgin. Hell, no. He has a past. So do I. I just never expected it to be thrown in my face like this.

I reach my car and my stomach lets out a growl. A couple lettuce leaves didn't do much for my hunger and I didn't have a chance to eat any of the meal Chance offered. The clock on my dash flashes seven. I can't go home. My bed sheets smell like Miles. Of what we did together.

I drive away from Bridger Ranch, away from Bayfield, ending up in Silverton. I pull up in front of the all-too-familiar roadside bar. Maybe I'm a masochist because this place also reminds me of Miles. But Tracy is working tonight and I could use my BFF.

When I pull into the lot, it's clear Saturday night is bustling at Jody's, as usual. I grab an empty seat at the bar.

"Hey, Sadie." Desiree, one of the bartenders, slides a cocktail napkin in front of me. "What sounds good tonight?"

Miles Bridger on a platter. If he weren't such a dickhead.

So then maybe just his head.

"Nothing too strong. I'm driving. How about a glass of Chardonnay?" I glance around. "Where's Tracy?"

"Right behind you."

I turn on my stool. "Hey, Trace!"

Tracy gives me a quick hug and then turns to Desiree. "I need three vodka tonics, Des."

"You got it." Desiree pours me a glass of Chard and then gets to work on the drinks for Tracy's table.

I take a sip of the crisp oaky wine. "I need one of your burgers."

"You got it. Medium rare with all the fixings?"

"You know it."

"I'll tell Andy. By the way, did you happen to see the new bartender?"

"Just Desiree." I gaze down the bar. "And Hank."

"The new guy must be on break." Tracy smiles and waves her diamond ring in my face. "If I weren't spoken for, I'd be all over him."

"Good thing you're spoken for."

"Well...he's also gay. And awesome. Oh! Here he comes. Let me introduce you." She nods to a dark-haired man who appears behind the bar. "Hey, Jake. Come here."

Jake ambles toward us, a rakish smile on his handsome face. "Tracy, how's our most beautiful waitress tonight?"

Tracy blushes. She's engaged and madly in love with Troy, but she fucking blushes, even if she doesn't stand a chance with the guy.

But when I take a long look at Jake, I can't say I blame her. He's muscled and gorgeous, and he's wearing a yellow button down. And damn if it doesn't work for him. If he's got a boyfriend, that guy is one lucky man.

"I want you to meet my friend Sadie. Sadie, this is Jake Garcia."

"Hey, Sadie." Jake holds his hand across the bar.

I give it a firm shake. "Nice to meet you, Jake."

"I'm putting in an order for a burger for Sadie," Tracy

says. "Will you make sure she gets it when it's ready? She's my bestie and I want you to take good care of her."

A wink accompanies his smile.

"Absolutely," Jake drawls. "I'll take real good care of you, Miss Sadie."

Tracy leaves and Jake cocks a hip on his side of the bar and studies me.

"Man troubles?" he asks.

My eyebrows wing up. "How can you tell?"

"I've had them before myself. I know the look."

I sigh. "Let's just say I thought I caught a good one, but I had to set him free."

"Catch and release, huh?"

I laugh. "You got it."

One of the cooks appears behind the bar. "Got a burger here, medium rare with everything plus fries."

Jake takes the plate from him. "Got it. Thanks. This one's yours, right?" He places it in front of me. "Need another drink to go with that, gorgeous?"

I glance at my wine glass. It's almost empty. "Just water. I'm driving."

"You are one good girl, aren't you?"

"Yup, I follow the rules."

"No adrenaline junkie then."

"Jake, my whole life is about adrenaline. I'm a cop."

His brows nearly jump off his forehead. "No way."

"Way." I take a bite of my burger. A little juice drips down my chin and I swipe it away with a napkin. "Which probably explains why I follow the rules."

"You don't look like any cop I've seen." His dark gaze rakes over me.

"You want to see my badge?"

He grins. "I bet most men want to see your handcuffs."

I shove another bite of burger in my mouth as I roll my eyes. Jake has no idea. While Miles wasn't interested in restraints, I could see him getting kinky. That night was so hot. And amazing. I frown.

"Let me take care of a few drinks and I'll come back and you can tell me *all* about this guy of yours."

13

$\mathcal{M}$ILES

"I'LL HAVE some more of that MacAllan now," I tell Chance, once I'm able to think straight after that damned text.

"Where's Sadie?" Austin holds up his glass of scotch.

"Went home," I say gruffly. *And she's probably never coming back.*

"What's the story with you two?" Chance asks.

"No story." *Not any longer, anyway.*

"Now that's a damned lie." Austin sips his drink. "You'd have to be blind not to see something's up with you two."

"Where's Carly?"

"Nice subject change," Austin says. "She went out to the kennels to check on Duchess and the pups."

"So speak freely." Chance puts his feet on the coffee table. "It's just us guys."

"Want me to do your nails now or straighten your hair?"

He glares.

I glare back. "Got nothing to say. Except I'll have some of that good stuff." I point to his drink.

"Is your arm broken?" Chance scoffs. "Get it yourself."

The bottle is on the coffee table, but I walk to the bar to retrieve a glass. I return to the couch, plunk my ass down, and pour half a finger of scotch.

"That's all you want?" Austin asks.

"I'm not much of a drinker." I want to get shit-faced, but that's not going to solve anything.

"The right woman can turn any man into a drinker for the night," Austin says. "Spill it."

"Nothing to spill."

"Have it your way." Austin finishes his scotch and rises. "I'm going to go to the kennels and see if Carly wants to take a walk."

"A walk back to your bedroom?" Chance says.

Austin laughs, shaking his head as he ambles toward the back door.

I take a small sip of the scotch. I like Chance, but I'm closer to Austin. Which is ridiculous because I don't know either one of them from Adam. But Austin and I are in the same boat. We were both uprooted from our lives and forced to come out here to bumfuck Montana. For Chance, nothing changed—except having two older brothers to boss around, which he genuinely seems to love doing. My aches have aches.

I sit silently, nursing the drink, until—

"She's a nice girl. Sadie." Chance sips his drink.

"Yeah."

"I don't know her that well. She just moved here a little over a year ago. I first met her at the pool hall. She plays a mean game."

"Great." Just what I need, to know more about Sadie. The woman who clearly hates my guts. I don't blame her because...shit. Rhonda and her fucking text.

"She might be there now." Chance cuts into my thoughts. "Over at Mikey's. Do you play?"

"Pool? I'm okay."

Which is damned lie. I'm great at pool. My mother's third husband was a pool shark and he taught me everything he knew. Applied geometry, he called it. Lloyd was the one husband of hers I liked and who liked me. He made a good living as an architect, and on the weekends, he cleaned up playing pool. Except the one time he got out-hustled and lost a bundle. Mom showed him the door after that...but not before she took him to the cleaners.

"Feel like heading into town?" he asks.

"How much have you had to drink?"

"Just one beer before dinner and a finger of scotch, which is nothing for my size. I'm good."

"I've got to make a call."

"Suit yourself."

Except Sadie might be there...

But no. I have to call Rhonda and get this shit figured out. We had sex, but it's been a while. Months. She didn't say how pregnant she is, an important detail.

Hell, I should have done it as soon as I got the text. The first one. Then Sadie wouldn't have seen it and my life wouldn't be a clusterfuck right now.

I rise. "Maybe another time."

Once I'm in the privacy of my bedroom, I make the dreaded call.

"Hello?"

"Rhonda?"

"Yeah. Hi, Miles."

"I got your text."

"And it took you this long to call back?"

"Yeah, it did. You kind of dropped a bomb on me."

"I've been trying to get in touch with you about it."

"I know, but we are long over and I never expected...

this. Besides, I'm suddenly a rancher, and then..." I plunk down onto my bed. "It's a long story."

"I heard. The short story is I'm pregnant. What do we do about it?"

I sigh. I can't do anything about it. The child is growing in her body, so it's her choice, but I sure as hell can make sure it's mine before I think about anything.

"How far along are you?"

"Four months."

I run the numbers in my head.

I breathe out a sigh of relief.

Then I get angry.

Yeah, Rhonda and I hooked up, but there was snow on the ground. I remember that because I left my coat behind and it was fucking freezing. It rarely snow in New York after March. That means the baby's not mine.

"You going to say anything?" she asks.

"Yeah, just a minute." I walk to my desk and sit down in front of my computer. I type in "paternity test in early pregnancy."

"Yes!" I say, louder than I mean to.

"Yes, what?"

"Sorry. We can do a non-invasive paternity test. A simple blood draw for you and a cheek swab for me."

"Are you kidding me, Miles? You want me to do a paternity test?"

"Well...yeah. I want to know for sure that the kid is mine, Rhonda." *Because it's not.*

"And my word isn't good enough for you?" she screeches.

"I'm no mathematician, but I sure as shit can't be that baby's father if you're four months along. What do you really want?"

"Miles," she sputters.

"You said you heard I'm a rancher now. That means you heard why I moved to Montana. Let me guess. From Dave at the shop who gave you my number. Probably the real father."

Her huff comes through the phone line clear as day.

"You want the money. *Jesus.* You're a piece of work, using your baby to get your hands on some cash."

She doesn't say anything, so I plow on.

"You've got two choices. Take the paternity test and prove I'm the father. Or fuck off."

"Fuck you!" She ends the call. Just as I thought.

Christ. What a total nightmare. No wonder Chance is single. He must be scared of being trapped by a gold digger just by sinking his dick into a woman.

Hell, who could blame the man?

Sadie isn't like that. She didn't know who I was when we first hooked up. And now she thinks I'm some rando's baby daddy. We couldn't have had a rockier start to a relationship—if it could ever be considered one after all the ups and downs we've been through in such a short time. I want to hunt her down, but I have no clue where to go.

Yes, I do.

I stalk back out of my bedroom and find Chance with his jacket on heading out the door.

"Where are you off to?"

"I told you. I feel like a game of pool."

"I changed my mind. I'm in."

———

MIKEY'S POOL Hall is a large warehouse, probably used to store crops before transport back in the day. The interior walls are brick and the ceiling is high and thick-beamed. It's got at least eight pool tables. Five of them are occupied.

"Fuck. Seriously?" I nudge Chance.

Mark Peterson is playing with a couple other men on the table closest to the bar.

Damn. Just what we need.

"Chance!" The guy behind the bar waves.

Chance walks toward him, and I follow, perfectly content to avoid Peterson and his overblown ego.

"Evening, Jed. This is my brother Miles."

The man—Jed, apparently—holds out his hand. "Good to meet you. So you're one of the billion heirs?"

Is there anyone in town who doesn't know about the inheritance? "Not quite yet," I reply.

"Can I get you two anything?"

"Tonic water for me," I say.

"Me, too." Chance turns to me. "I play lousy when I'm drinking."

"You got it." Jed pours our drinks.

"Put it on my tab." Chance grabs the icy glasses and passes one to me. "We're going to take table six."

"Enjoy." Jed turns to another customer.

Chance and I head to the table, and I ignore the glare from Peterson. I don't have it in me to deal with him tonight.

"How are you at eight-ball?" Chance asks.

"Okay."

I take a look at the table. Four by eight. Regulation size. Most pool halls have smaller seven-foot tables. I look for a coin slot and find none. It's free to play. Strange. Whoever Mikey is, he clearly owns this place outright and earns his keep off the drinks.

"You want to break?" I ask.

"I'll rack." Chance grabs the triangle. "You do the honors."

I scan the pool cues on the wall and weigh a few in my

hands until I find the one that feels right. I chalk the tip and break, sending the five ball into a side pocket.

"Guess I'm solids," I say.

I continue to pocket solids and then the eight ball to successfully obliterate Chance in the first game before he even gets a turn.

"What the hell?" My brother stares at the table, eyes wide. "You said you were"—air quote—"*okay?*"

"One of my mom's husbands was a hustler." I rack the balls for the second game. "Taught me everything I know."

"You know hustling's illegal, right?" he mutters.

"Did I ask you to play for money?"

"Sorry. I guess I should have mentioned that Peterson over there is kind of a staple at Mikey's. He's known as the best pool player in town."

I chuckle. "So?"

"*He* hustles here, although not much any longer since he's run out of people to take money from. The cop bends the rules to suit himself. Man, it'd piss him off if you beat his ass. He's undefeated as far as I know."

This time I grin. I can see the interest in Chance's voice to take the fucker down a notch or two. "Until now," I reply.

"Bro, you want to break the law with a cop?"

"I can't hustle for *money,*" I clarify.

"What the hell is going on in that warped mind of yours?"

"I'm not sure yet. But maybe we can get him off our backs."

Chance shakes his head. "That's a bad idea. Peterson is still the law around here."

"So I spend a night in jail. Shankle can bail my ass out. It would be worth it."

Chance grins. "Yeah, it fucking would. But then Peterson will be so far up our asses we won't be able to shit right."

He has a point. "Fine. It's your turn to break." I rack the balls.

"I think I need a handicap."

"Sorry, bro. No can—" I stop mid-sentence.

"What?" Then Chance follows my gaze to the entrance.

Sadie's here. Still wearing that damned black miniskirt.

And she's not alone.

14

—————

THE POOL HALL IS BUSY. I scan the place like a good cop should as soon as I enter. I take in two things—or rather, two people—at once. Not things, people.

Mark's here, but that's not a surprise. Only annoying.

And Miles is here. With his brother Chance.

Shit. My heart leaps at the sight of him and then drops back into place. Back to reality. Why the hell is he here?

Sometimes I really hate small towns.

I stop short and Jake sets his hand on my shoulder instead of bumping into me. Miles's gaze settles on that action and his jaw clenches.

Jake leans in. "He's here, isn't he?"

I nod and move toward the bar. "Yeah."

I didn't want to see him tonight. After my burger, I was going to head home, but Jake could tell I didn't want to be alone with my thoughts, although I shared too many of them with him. I don't know how he wrangled it, but he left his shift early to hang with me. Since Tracy couldn't get off like he did, I'm thankful to hang with someone instead of crying through a pity party of one in my apartment.

Jake's nice. Funny. And he's the only guy I've met who understands the struggle with dating men. So I spilled it all to him and he told me to stop running. To face Miles head-on, because if I wanted something with him, I needed to put my big-girl panties on and deal with the issues.

Of course, he didn't say big-girl panties. He said to grow a pair. Either way, I wasn't planning to do it *now*.

I'm angry that Miles got a woman pregnant. The guy I slept with, who I thought I shared a connection with, has baby drama. I don't want that. But the fling happened before I knew him. It didn't even happen in this state. It was before me.

I can't hold past encounters against him. I sure don't want him holding mine against me.

Still, it hurts. And Jake's right. I ran. I saw that text, heard Miles confirm it happened, and bolted.

The music switches to Stevie Ray Vaughan as Jake and I order drinks.

"Sadie."

My heart skips a beat at the deep sound of Miles's voice. I flick my gaze to Jake's and turn around. There, almost too close, stands Miles.

I breathe in his scent. Take in the rasp of whiskers on his square jaw. His narrowed gaze burns into me.

"Hey," I say. "This is Jake."

Miles holds his hand out and Jake shakes it, a big grin splitting his face.

"Miles. How's it hanging?"

Once Miles releases his grasp, he sets his hand on my waist and steers me down the long bar. He leans in and murmurs. "Want to tell me why the hell you're here with another man? After I woke up in your bed this morning?"

My cheeks heat furiously. I step away from his touch. "Jake's my friend. How's the baby-naming going?"

His eyes narrow. "The baby's not mine."

I cross my arms over my chest. "Oh, yeah? Rhonda seems to think so."

He runs a hand over his face. "She seems to think I'm an idiot, too. She heard about the will. About the inheritance. She wanted to cash in."

I blink. "What?"

"The first but probably not the last of annoying people trying to use me for shit." He pins me with his intense eyes. "Yes, I did sleep with her, Sadie. I admitted to that earlier."

I blink. Listen.

"A one-night stand back in the winter. She consented and knew the score. That it wasn't anything more than one time. Didn't spend the night. Hell, I didn't even know her last name. I still wouldn't except she gave it to me in the text."

"Just a release." I roll my eyes.

I'm not really thrilled to know that Miles thinks so little of his bedmates, but it's not wrong. I've had flings before–there was a time when I didn't want a relationship, just some orgasms.

What I'm feeling is jealousy, plain and simple. Another woman got to sleep with him. To touch him. To know what it feels like to lie beneath him.

"Just a release," he echoes.

His blue eyes sear into mine. I try to push down my jealousy. Rhonda is in New York—I think—and he clearly wants nothing to do with her.

"She said she was four months along. It's been longer than that since we were together. So I told her I wanted a paternity test."

"That didn't go well, you telling her that?"

He shakes his head. "I'm not a mathematician, but clearly neither is she. The baby was probably made with a guy I employ. *Used* to employ. My guess is they got it in their heads to get me to pay her off using the billion I'm going to inherit."

"Is there actually a baby or did they only hatch a scheme?"

He shrugs those broad shoulders. "I have no idea. Don't rightfully care."

"I'm sorry." I look to the floor and then back to Miles. "For more than you being used like that. I shouldn't have run."

I glance over my shoulder. Jake is still standing at the bar, chatting with a few people around him.

Miles shifts to look at him as well. "Right into another man's arms."

I see how it looks, how an alpha guy like him could be angry. Jealous. "Jake's just a friend."

Jake looks up and gives me a wink.

"You sure about that?" Miles asks.

A guy comes in the door, looks around, and spots Jake. Heads his way. Gives him a kiss.

"Pretty sure," I reply.

Miles grins. "Yeah, I guess he's not my competition."

I shake my head and laugh.

"We're a couple of hotheads, aren't we?" Miles says.

I sigh. "Yes. I think we need to take some time to get to know each other."

"All I have is time, sweetheart, but there's some heavy shit that keeps getting in the way." He reaches out and tucks my hair behind my ear.

I crave that touch, and I grasp his wrist and give it a squeeze. "Lots of heavy shit."

"Hopkins!"

We turn at Mark's voice.

"Oh, fuck. What now?" Miles grumbles.

Peterson approaches. Instead of his usual weekend swagger, his gaze is hard. Sharp. His shoulders are back. Cop mode.

"Got a call from the coroner." He waggles his cell in the air.

"Now?" Miles says.

Peterson looks up at him, nods. "We put a rush on the autopsy of the body from the creek and the coroner thought this might not want to wait until Monday."

I frown and glance up at Miles.

Miles sets his hand on my back. "If you're going to tell me I have something to do with the murder, we're going to have a problem, Peterson."

He gives Miles a quick glance and shakes his head. Then he looks at me. "I feel confident you're off the hook, Bridger. She dates the murder to a couple months ago."

That doesn't clear Chance, but I see Miles deflate a little out of relief. It looks like Mark has more to say.

"What else is there?" Miles asks.

I nod. "Yes. What did she find?"

"The body..." He heaves out a sigh and looks at me. "The body has been identified as Joseph Hopkins. DNA matches yours on file."

My mouth falls open.

My brother. Joey. He's the dead guy in the creek. On the Bridger property.

"From when he disappeared." My voice is wooden. Numb. I'm trying to process what the hell that all means.

Peterson nods.

Oh. My. God.

I lean into Miles unintentionally, but I'm thankful for his size and strength. All my hope of ever finding Joey is gone.

"Joseph Hopkins?" A frown mars Miles's brow. "The body is someone in your family?"

I nod.

I swallow. "My brother. I guess he came back from Canada. Or he never went at all."

15

M ILES

SADIE'S PEACHES-AND-CREAM complexion has gone stark white, and I wrap my arms around her to steady her. "Easy, baby."

She grips the bar.

I've been a fucking idiot. A caveman who dragged his woman back to his cave and took possession. When I saw her come in with that guy... Yeah, I lost my shit.

Sadie is mine.

I don't have any claim on her. We barely know each other, but whenever we're together, the chemistry is intense. Being with her settles something inside me. And obviously riles me the fuck up.

We've spent most of our time since we met being mad at each other. It seems like everything is a total shit show right now. And we're barely keeping our heads above all the mess.

And now this. The worst of all.

Her brother's dead. On our ranch. Killed by someone.

"Listen, Hopkins," Peterson says, clearly trying—and failing—to look contrite. "I didn't mean to lay this on you like that."

Without letting go of Sadie, I turn my gaze on him. "The hell you didn't. It's Saturday night, for God's sake. We're at a pool hall, not on the fucking clock. Did you even know about her brother?"

He shrugs. "No. I mean, maybe. Yeah, she might have mentioned it. That's how she decided to enter the police academy."

"I'm okay, Miles," Sadie says against my shoulder.

Thank fuck she believes me about Rhonda and the baby. I want to be here for her and have nothing like that mess between us. Not any longer. The fact that she's seeking comfort in me is proof she's let it go. Or that she needs me no matter what clusterfuck stands in our way.

"You're a piece of work, Peterson." I shake my head.

"Look." Peterson clears his throat. "This is just as big a surprise to me as it is to any of you."

"Doubtful," I add.

"But crime doesn't take time off. Did you want me to wait until Monday morning to tell you?" he asks Sadie.

"No. I'm glad you told me. I'm just...surprised."

He nods, clearly satisfied by his action now that Sadie has validated it.

"I'm going to need to know, Bridger. Did your father have any dealings with Joseph Hopkins?" His question is aimed my way, lobbed like a grenade.

"Like I'd know!" I snap. "How many times do I have to tell you? I never even met the bastard."

"What's going on here?"

I turn to see my half brother, barrel-chested and huge, join us. He has his usual pissed-off look on his face and it's well aimed at Peterson.

"Bridger," Peterson says.

"Detective." Chance waves to Jed and jiggles his empty glass.

"I was just telling Miles and Sadie here that we got the ID on the body at your place."

Jed hands Chance a refill on his tonic water, and Chance takes a sip. He glances at me and then at Sadie, who's in my arms. If he's surprised to see her in my embrace, he doesn't show it.

"Don't keep me in suspense," Chance says.

"It's Joseph Hopkins. Sadie's brother." Peterson darts arrows at Chance with his eyes. "I don't suppose *you'd* know anything about that?"

Chance looks to Sadie, his face softening. "Shit, sweetheart. I'm real sorry to hear that." Then he glances back at Peterson, all kindness stripped away. "We've been over this before. I don't like what you're insinuating—that I had anything to do with it, a relation of Sadie's or not." Chance gulps down the rest of his tonic.

I don't like what Peterson's laying down either. Chance may be a giant pain in my ass but he's a good man. A damned good man. There's no way he'd kill someone.

Sadie is still glommed onto me, and I have to admit, she feels damned good in my arms. I like comforting her, when we're not pissed at each other for stupid shit. But this? Her missing brother dead on *our* land? That's not stupid shit. It's a big fucking deal, and one hell of a coincidence.

Damn, the feelings she's bringing out in me... It's disturbing...and I like it. I like it a lot. She didn't tell me a lot about her brother, just that he was ten years older and they weren't close. That she hadn't seen him in years.

"Like it or not," Peterson goes on, "that body was found on your property. It will be investigated to the fullest extent of the law. Sadie's brother deserves justice."

"How do you know—" I stop abruptly.

I was about to ask whether Joseph Hopkins might have taken his own life. Glad I stopped myself. Sadie doesn't need to hear that theory. There's also no reason he would kill himself on Bridger land.

"Cause of death?" Chance asks.

"Per the coroner, unclear," Peterson says. "Establishing cause and manner of death in a body recovered from water is usually a challenge. She estimates it's been three to four months since death, so if there were any substances in his system at the time of his death, toxicology won't show it now."

"So if he was drugged, we won't know," Chance says.

Peterson nods. The sounds of the pool hall circle around us. The crack of the balls. The twangy guitar music. Low voices.

"Right. But the exam didn't show any outward signs of drug use."

Sadie sinks farther into me, and she chokes out a sob.

"This conversation is over." I shake my head. "You think you can have this talk somewhere besides three feet from the deceased's sister?" I kiss the top of her head.

"She's a detective on the case," he counters.

"If you thought there was a conflict of interest before," I say, "she's up to her eyeballs in it now. I'd say she's off the case."

Sadie doesn't say anything, which says a lot because she and I can argue too fucking easily.

"Baby, let's go," I murmur.

Sadie looks up at me, and I swear all I want to do is take her home and protect her forever from everything in the world. Peterson. This case. Even shit like Rhonda.

Damn.

"I'm okay, Miles," she whispers.

Except she's not okay. Her gorgeous lips are turned down into a frown, and her eyes are glistening with unshed tears.

"I'm taking you home."

Sadie sniffles. "I've got my car. Jake drove himself."

Oh yeah. Jake. He can just fucking deal.

"I'll take you home in your car."

Sadie fishes in her purse and then hands me her key fob.

This means I don't have a ride back from her place, but maybe that's what she's intending.

I hope that's what she's intending, anyway. All I want to do is take care of this woman. Hold her. Run her a hot bath and wash her beautiful skin.

My God, I've never wanted that before. I'm not selfish and always putting my needs first, but as far as women are concerned, my MO has always been to fuck and forget.

Before now. Before Sadie.

Now it's not just about sex—although that's the most amazing thing—but the whole package. I care about Sadie, and seeing her hurting hurts me.

"We're going to need to meet in my office first thing Monday morning," Peterson says.

"Are you talking to me or to your partner?" My voice isn't kind.

"Both of you. Chance and Sadie. You and Austin are cleared. Nine a.m. sharp, Monday."

Chance grunts and narrows his gaze.

"I'll be there. No way Sadie's handling this alone," I tell him.

"My lawyer Shankle's not as pretty as Sadie, but he'll be there, too," Chance adds. "He'll be representing her as well."

Damned straight. Sadie isn't rolling in cash like the Bridgers. Or like we will be. No way is she getting anything but the best. Shankle might be annoying, but he knows his stuff.

With Austin and me off Peterson's list, I can focus better. Honestly, though? My biggest concern right now is Sadie.

That body is her brother. *Was* her brother.

Her fucking brother, dead on our property. Is there no end to what my esteemed father was capable of? The havoc he wreaked? He *has* to be the one responsible for this mess. But why? How? How was he connected to Sadie's brother?

These are questions Peterson is smart enough to figure out, or we'll have to do it for him.

I walk Sadie out of the pool hall, my arm around her securely. I click the key fob, and we head toward the flashing lights of her car.

Sadie drives a green VW Beetle. I don't know why, but that simple fact makes me smile, even though I know my long legs are going to be scrunched up in that front seat.

I open the passenger side door and help her get in, and then I enter the car on the driver's side. It's a manual transmission.

Sadie drives a stick. That's really cool. A small thing, but I fall even harder for her in that moment.

The drive to her place only takes a few minutes since Bayfield is so fucking small, and I help her out of the car. Lead her into her apartment, unlocking the door with the keys I didn't give back.

"What can I do for you?" I ask once we're inside her apartment.

It looks just as I left it this morning. When I left in anger. When she held off on telling Peterson about us until she was forced to.

I take a deep breath, realize I'm a fucking hypocrite. Chance obviously knows I'm into Sadie after the pool hall.

I still haven't told him, even earlier when both he and Austin asked what's between us.

I suck at relationships. Or do I? I've never actually had one to suck at. But yeah. This *is* one, even if I'm doing a really good job of fucking it all up. Again and again. First by getting pissed she wanted to keep us a secret. Then by letting my past with Rhonda get in the way. If the tables were turned and Sadie told me she was pregnant because of a past fling, I'd be pissed too, even if it happened before I knew her. Pregnancy mistakes happen, man or woman.

Then there was my jealousy and how I thought she moved on to Jake. Her gay friend.

I need to get my head on straight. Stop fucking up. Sadie was hurt. Surprised. Stunned. I can't be a dick— even unintentionally—now.

She lifts her dark gaze to mine. "I don't know. But don't go. Please. I don't want to be alone."

"Absolutely. Would you like me to make you some coffee? Tea?" I've never made tea, but how difficult can it be to dunk a bag into hot water?

Her dark hair slides over her shoulders as she shakes her head. "No. Maybe just some water."

I walk into her small kitchen, search the cupboards for a glass, and fill it from the tap, adding a cube of ice from the freezer. I take it to her. She's seated on her loveseat, so

I settle next to her and hand her the glass. She nods her thanks and then takes a long sip.

"I'm so sorry, baby." I lift my arm to wrap it around her shoulders.

"It's weird." She stares blankly toward her bookcase. "I don't really know how to feel. We were estranged. When my parents got divorced, Joey was already eighteen, and he went off with my father, supposedly to work construction for his company. I haven't seen or heard from either of them in...years."

"Still, he's your brother." I temper my voice to be as gentle as possible.

"*Was* my brother."

I wish I could take every ounce of sadness out of Sadie and bear it myself. I've only had brothers for a couple of weeks, but I sure as hell don't want to lose one of them.

The thought surprises me, that Chance and Austin have become important to me. If that can happen in two weeks, I can't even imagine what Sadie's going through, estranged or not.

Of course, we've been dealing with one thing after another since we got here. Austin finding Carly, dealing with her horrid past and her overbearing father, the mess between that guy and our father.

Our father.

Our father.

It all leads back to him.

And now Sadie's pulled into this shit.

She takes another sip of her water, and I wrap my arm around her shoulders. I want to ask her again what I can do for her, but I risk repeating myself and sounding more helpless than I feel. Maybe she just needs me to be here.

She finishes her water and then leans into me, nuzzling her head against my shoulder, reminding me of how much smaller she is. Fragile.

We sit there.

We sit there for a long time with only the sound of the fridge and a car driving by coming through the window.

My cock is hyper aware of the beautiful woman next to me, and it reacts in kind. The feel of her. Her scent. I force myself to ignore it all. No, not ignore—absorb, but don't act upon it.

I appreciate every bit that is my woman.

Yeah, my fucking woman.

The old Miles might have taken advantage of the situation, advantage of a woman's neediness.

I won't do that to Sadie. I care about this woman. Odd, as part of me never imagined caring about any woman. But Sadie Hopkins has somehow managed to get under my skin, and she's inching toward my heart.

It's a scary thought, yet it's not scary at the same time.

Part of it feels as natural to me as rebuilding a transmission on a bike.

Is this what love is? Is this what Austin feels for Carly? Is this why he braved her crazy father and that storm and everything else? I haven't known Sadie long enough to even think about love... Have I?

I kiss the top of her head and inhale the fragrant scent of her hair. Raspberries and vanilla.

She pulls away from me slightly and sets the glass on an end table. Then she turns to me, her eyes sunken and sad.

"Miles?"

"Yes?"

"Take me to bed. Please."

16

$\mathcal{S}$ADIE

MILES HELPS ME INTO A STAND, and for some reason, I start talking. It's been a crazy night. From the fight to his jealousy to learning about Joey... It's all so surreal.

I'm not alone in this though. Deep down, maybe I knew Joey was dead but couldn't admit it. There was no news from him for so long. I never understood why we were estranged, why he wouldn't want to talk to me, his baby sister.

But I held out hope. Maybe having him gone is better. Now I know he doesn't hate me, isn't avoiding me because I did something. Except...I don't want him gone.

"My best memory of Joey is from when I was five years old. A big snowstorm came through. Nothing new around here. Once it was over, snow was piled high in huge drifts around Larson Hill. Joey and his friends were going sledding, and I wanted to go so badly. Mom said I was too young, that I wouldn't be able to stay warm enough, but Joey took one look at me, his eyes smiling."

I continue talking as my memory hurls backward and the scene becomes vivid in my mind. I can't help but smile.

"I'll take care of her, Ma. Let her go."

My mom twists her lips. "I don't know, Joe. She's awfully little."

"I know how to keep her warm." Joey goes to the closet and pulls out my purple snowsuit and then he disappears for a moment and returns with one of my sweaters and two pairs of his socks. He pushes the sweater over my head, and I laugh when he tousles my messed-up hair.

"I need two old bread bags, Ma," he says.

Ma brings them to him while Joey gets me into my snowsuit, slides my stocking cap onto my head and then wraps a woolen scarf around me so only my nose is sticking out. He takes one pair of socks and puts them on my hands, pulling them up over the sleeves of my snowsuit nearly to my elbows. He shoves my mittens on my hands after that. I can't move my thumbs but I don't care. He takes the other pair of socks, slides them onto my little feet, and then makes me step into the plastic bread bags and then into my boots.

"Look at that, Ma," he says. "How can she not stay warm?"

Ma laughs. "All right, Joe. But you bring her back in one piece, and not frozen."

"Will do."

"That afternoon," I tell Miles, "with the sun shining down on the sparkling snow, and Joey and his two friends taking turns pulling me on the sled, is still one of my best memories."

He chuckles. "Could you even move in that getup?"

I shake my head and can't help the small chuckle. "Not really, but I didn't have to move. I just had to stay on the sled."

Miles's eyes crinkle at the corner as he gives me a smile. "That sounds great, baby. I wish I'd had a little sister to take sledding."

I warm at the thought. Miles would have been a great big brother. Protective and bossy, but in a good way.

"Central Park was always too crowded," he continues, "but sometimes I went upstate with my grandmother."

"Did you?" He hasn't mentioned anyone in his family before besides his mom. The woman who was Jonathan Bridger's second wife.

"Yeah. Until my mom alienated her, too," he grumbles.

Funny. When my mom and dad divorced when I was eight and Joey was eighteen, Mom got custody of me, and I hardly saw my father or brother after that. My dad stopped being my dad, and it's been a long time since I've seen him. He lives outside Billings in tiny house, and last I heard he's pretty much a drunk.

But what I went through sounds tame compared to Miles's life. It can't be more obvious how his father wanted nothing to do with him. Or Austin. And what of Chance? They lived together on the ranch but from what I see, Chance hates the guy just as much. Maybe more.

I don't let myself dwell on the memory of Joey often, as it makes me miss him, makes me sad at what I've lost. When I found out he'd disappeared, it was a brick to my gut. Now that I know he's gone for good? That memory is all I have, and I want to hold it close to my heart. Joey will always be the big brother who took me sledding on that wonderful snowy afternoon.

"What do you need?" Miles asks. "You want me to start the shower for you?"

"Yeah. I want to wash this day away."

"Oh, baby, I wish I could wash the day away for you, especially any part where I made you sad or upset. But life doesn't work that way."

"I just wish I knew what he was doing." I sigh. "If he was hauling freight to Canada, how did he get on your property? And if he wasn't hauling freight, which I'm betting he wasn't, then what *was* he doing? How did he...*die?*"

"You heard Peterson. It's going to be difficult to find the cause of death. There was clearly no blunt trauma, and it's been too long for toxicology to be accurate with his body."

I can't help a wince. Thinking of my brother as "a body" feels all kinds of wrong.

He sighs and pulls me close. "Fuck. I'm sorry, Sadie. I shouldn't have said any of that."

I cling to him once more. "It's okay. It's the truth. Just hard to hear. I don't want to talk about it anymore. He's gone. He's been gone, but now we can find answers. I'll have to face it soon enough. We both will, even though you're no longer a suspect and, as you told Peterson, I'm probably no longer on the case. Peterson doesn't expect to see us until Monday, but I know who we can talk to for answers."

"Who?" His brows draw together as he strokes my hair.

"My father."

"You know where he is?"

I nod. "I've got a pretty good idea."

"Okay. Tomorrow, we'll go see him."

Good. Tomorrow will come soon enough. "For tonight though, I need to let it go."

He nods and brings my fingers to his lips, kisses the tips. "Okay. I understand."

Miles. Strong and protective Miles.

Miles, who didn't get another woman pregnant after all. Who wasn't involved in my brother's death. Who's here right now for me.

Miles turns the shower on for me, and I slowly peel my clothes from my body, completely uninhibited.

When I stand naked, his eyes flare and his jaw clenches. He rakes his gaze over every inch of me, from my painted toenails to the top of my head. Then he turns and walks out of the bathroom.

"Miles," I say.

"I'll give you some privacy."

Privacy? To be alone? "No, wait. Please."

He turns around and he fixes his gaze to mine.

"I... I really can't be alone."

"I'm not going anywhere. I'll wait for you in your living room."

I swallow. I don't even want him *that* far away. "Join me? In the shower?"

"Sadie..."

"Please, Miles. I need you. I need to feel alive."

He studies me some more, as if looking for some mystery. "Are you sure?"

"Standing here naked, right in front of you, I'm absolutely sure. Shower with me. Stay with me. Tonight. In my bed. Make me forget."

17

M ILES

I WAS TRYING to do the right thing. Give her room. Space. Allow her to process the news of her brother's death without any pressure or expectation from me.

So I don't push her to do anything. She wants a drink, I get her a drink. She wants a shower, I turn the hot water on. That's it.

I want nothing from her. I want to give.

But when she *wants* me to touch her, to give her pleasure so she forgets, I will do that too. Not because my dick is hard and I know how perfectly tight and wet her pussy is. How I can get lost in her...

No. I want her to get lost in *me*. She's seeking solace in my hands. In my body. I'm the only one who can do this for her.

It's my privilege.

I'll see it done. Even if I don't come, if I have blue balls for the rest of the ·night, I'll see her sated and her mind empty.

When I nod, she steps into the shower and her body is surrounded by swirling steam.

I strip as she watches, and then she holds out her wet hand for me. I close the door behind me and join her beneath the spray, turning us so my back blocks the water. Grabbing her a bar of soap, I rub it between my palms to work up a thick lather.

We don't say anything as I clean every inch of her silky skin. Shoulders. Arms. Back. Breasts. Belly. I drop to my knees and wash her legs, and them I move up to her pussy.

My touch is careful but I can't help but be possessive. Every curve of her is mine and I revel in her beauty.

One small hand settles on my shoulder. Her breathing picks up and she shudders slightly. The water pounds my back, drips down my face as I look up at her.

She doesn't say anything, only nods. The water reaches her now and the suds are rinsed free.

With a hand at her hip, I press her back against the tile

and then lift a foot up onto the back lip of her tub. This opens her up and my hand on her steadies her.

Leaning in, I nudge her core first with the tip of my nose and then my tongue, lapping up the water and her wetness.

She tangles her fingers in my hair, tugging.

"Miles," she moans.

Her sweetness coats my tongue and I make it my mission, my goal, to get her off. My name is a plea. A beg.

She wants to come. Needs to come.

I'll use every bit of skill I possess to give it to her. I won't give it to her swiftly though. Perhaps it's what I should do, give her the release she craves. But she wants to forget as well. Bringing her to the brink of release and then retreating will clear her mind.

Make her think of nothing but the chance of an orgasm.

"Miles!" she shouts. This time, it's more desperate. Frantic.

I look up at her again. She's squirming against my face. Her hands are squeezing and clenching. Her head's thrown back, her breasts upturned.

Now's when she'll come. The first time.

I slide a finger into her slick heat and then out, searching for just the right spot. When she makes a mewling sound and her pussy clenches down, I know I've found it.

I suck on her hard little clit as I curl my finger, my free hand cupping her ass and keeping her right where I want her. I'm relentless now. Pushing and pushing until she has no choice but to break. To come all over my hand. My mouth.

Her scream echoes off the tile and is the perfect sound.

My dick is so hard, my balls ache. Pre-come that seeps from the slit is washed away. The spray actually hurts. But none of that matters.

"Again," I growl.

She shakes her head. "I can't," she whimpers, but her body tells a different story.

My finger's still inside her and at my command, she clenches again.

I flick my tongue out against her swollen clit.

"Oh my God." Her back curls inward, as if she's bringing herself closer to the pleasure.

It doesn't take much to push her over once more, her body so sensitive already.

She wilts into my hand and I stand, wrap my arms around her as she shakes and moans.

I turn off the water, grab a towel from outside the

shower, and rub her dry. Only then do we step out and I wrap a second one around my waist.

She's pliant and sleepy, her eyes barely open.

"Don't fall asleep on me now, sweetheart. I'm not done with you yet."

She doesn't say anything as I lead her to her bed, yank the covers back so they're out of the way, and settle her in the center. Crawling on top of her, I kiss her. I know she can taste herself on my tongue and she moans.

I lick any missed drops of water off her dewy skin, working my way down her neck, over her collarbones, to her breasts. I treasure one and then the other until she's writhing and moaning once again.

"More?" I nuzzle the soft underside of her breast.

"In me. *Now*," she growls.

A smile spreads across my face as I leave her to grab my jeans and pull out a condom. I don't waste a second, not wanting her to think about a thing.

I want to go bareback with her so fucking bad, but after the Rhonda incident, we haven't had a chance to talk about protection. I want her to know that I'll keep her safe, even in this.

When it's time for us to talk about it, we will, but with clear heads. And probably clothes on.

For now, this time, I'll do the thinking about this for both of us.

The package is torn open and the latex rolled down my length in seconds.

I settle between her parted thighs.

"Sadie, eyes on me."

Her lashes flutter open and her dark eyes meet mine.

"There's my girl."

Only then do I push into her in one smooth, long stroke.

Fuck, she's perfect.

"Made for me," I tell her. Whispering that and all kinds of things about how perfect she is, how she's mine. How I'm hers. Everything and nothing as we get lost in each other. Only when she's come again all over my dick do I finally allow myself to release.

She's asleep before I take care of the condom. I gather the blankets and cover us so she stays warm. She's safe in my arms.

Nothing will happen tonight. Tomorrow is soon enough for life to creep back in.

Tomorrow. When we meet her father.

18

___

*S*ADIE

THE SUN'S rays stream through my window, and I open my eyes.

For a moment, my mind is clear, my body satiated, and next to me is the man of my dreams.

I smile.

Then the previous evening careens back into my mind.

The body.

My brother's body.

Peterson.

My father.

I have to talk to my father. My mother too, of course. Then I have to wonder if the coroner or Peterson had someone sent to tell them of the news. They're the next of kin. Not me. The only reason I know is because I'm involved in the case.

Shit. Joey was estranged from Mom as well, so...I want to get to my dad first. Get answers. We all deserve them.

The drive to Billings will take us an hour.

Us. We. I'm assuming Miles will come with me.

I need him to come with me. I haven't seen or talked to my dad since I checked in with him about Joey when he first disappeared. Then nothing. No news from either of them. Years.

He might be the guy who made me, but he's nothing but a sperm donor for his lack of involvement in my life.

Miles is lying on his back, the sheet tented with his morning wood.

My smile returns. Maybe I can escape this day for just a few more moments by giving him the blowjob of a lifetime.

It's funny. I love men, but giving head has never been my favorite thing to do. So why do I want Miles's dick in my mouth so fucking bad?

I rise from the bed quietly, take a quick trip to the bathroom, and then pad to the kitchen to start a pot of coffee. Then I creep back into bed with Miles—who hasn't even stirred—and remove the covers from him.

God, he's a fucking work of art. His cock is smooth and gorgeous with one purple vein marbling through it. He's hard and ready, and I could easily sink down on him. I'm ready, just thinking about it. But I don't have any condoms in the apartment. I could rummage in his jeans to see if he has another. I'm on the pill and clean as a whistle, but we haven't talked about going bare and I don't want to take his choice about that from him.

So a blowjob it will be.

I lean down, flick the tip of my tongue over the head of his cock.

His eyes flutter open. "This is one hell of a way to wake up."

"Shh," I say, licking the crown like a lollipop. "Let me take care of you."

"You're the one who needs taking care of."

He begins to sit up, but I push at his chest and force him back down. He huffs out a laugh because I know he's allowing me to manhandle him. If he wants to do something, I physically can't stop him.

"Please," I whisper, gripping the base and stroking him from root to tip. "I need this. I want to do this for you."

He hisses and his hips involuntarily buck. "You sure?"

I nod and watch as a drop of liquid seeps from the slit. "God, I'm so sure."

He smiles, closes his eyes.

And I flick my tongue over his cock head once more, getting that salty essence.

He groans in a subtle vibration that I feel more than hear.

I suck at his broad head, and then I lick long strokes over his shaft before I take him completely—well, as much as I can—into my mouth.

Another groan pulsates through me, I'm not sure whether it came from Miles or from me.

I suck him as far back to my throat as I can, and then I ease up, only to begin again.

"Baby. Feels so good."

Yeah, it does. I'm hyper aware of the tingling between my legs. I continue to suck his dick, harder and faster, until his hands are in my hair, and he's moving with me, adjusting to my rhythm.

"God, Sadie. What a sweet fucking mouth you have."

His balls are tightening, and I know he's close to release. Will he come in my mouth? Do I want him to?

Fuck, yes. I want him to.

He has other ideas, though, as he springs forward, dislodging his cock from my lips, and with one swift movement, I'm flat on my back and he's hovering over me.

"Sorry, baby, but if I let you keep doing that, I was going to come, and I'm not ready to come yet."

In another flash, my legs are spread, and he's feasting between them.

Eating me. Devouring me. Taking me over the edge. And then again.

When I'm completely spent, he crawls forward, touches his lips gently to mine.

"Sadie," he murmurs. "My Sadie." He kisses me again, this time sliding his tongue into my mouth, letting me taste my own juices.

I run my hands over his muscled shoulders, his taut back, loving the warmth of him, his large size, his sheer strength.

I'm ready. So ready.

Ready for him to plunge into me, ease the empty ache inside me.

He breaks the kiss. "Baby..."

"Hmm?" I murmur against his stubble.

"I need to get a condom."

I nod. "Okay. But I'm on the pill. And clean."

"Fuck," he growls against my neck. "I'm clean too. I swear it. I had a physical right before I left New York. Damn. To feel you. To feel every inch of you with no barrier. Fuck. You sure?"

I nod.

He thrusts into me hard and swift, with a groan that shatters my soul.

"Shit. I've never gone bare with anyone before. You feel so good."

I feel something new in that instant, and it's not because he's inside me, and it's not because I'm in some kind of needy place.

It's because, in this timeless moment, I know, without a doubt, that this man completes me in a way I never imagined. Never conceived.

He thrusts into me hard and fast. No gentle loving like last night. This morning it's raw and feral.

And it's exactly what I need. I claw at him, hook my heels around his butt, pull him closer.

I come.

He comes, hot and thick inside me.

And when he stays inside for those few precious moments while our climaxes subside, I feel something foreign. Foreign and delectable.

I feel...*love*.

We lie there, joined, for a few more minutes before he rolls off me, his arm strewn over his eyes. "Damn, baby. God damn."

I snuggle into his shoulder. "Coffee's made."

He tips his head, eyes me. "How about we forget coffee and stay in bed all day?"

"God, I wish." I blow out a breath. "But I have to see my dad."

His mood visibly changes. "Right. We do."

I run my fingers through the smattering of hair on his chest. "Does that mean you're coming with me?"

He turns, meets my gaze. "Baby, there's no place I'd rather be than at your side today."

A few more minutes, and I disentangle myself from Miles. Sit up. "I should call him. Make sure he's home."

"You have his number?"

I nod, frown. "Yeah. His company number goes to his cell on weekends." I roll over to the side of the bed and grab my phone from the nightstand.

The last time I talked to him, I was enrolling in the academy. He hates cops, so I didn't tell him. I just said I was leaving college. He said it was a mistake. I told him he was entitled to his opinion and then hung up. Joey was missing. He didn't like my life choices. There was nothing else to talk about.

I draw in a breath and make the call.

It rings once. Twice. Three times. Four. I'm ready to give up when—

"Hello?" A female voice.

Not surprising.

"Hi. This is Sadie. I'm looking for my dad."

"Sadie? I don't know any Sadie."

"Is Curt there? Curtis Hopkins? This is his daughter."

"What the eff?" Then, muffled, "Curt. Phone for you. Some woman who says she's your daughter. Since when do you have a damned daughter?"

"Give me the phone, Rainey." Then an angry, "Yeah? This is Curt Hopkins."

"It's me, Dad. It's Sadie."

"What the hell do you want? Does your mother need money?"

Miles must be able to hear his voice through the phone, because he sets his hand on my thigh and strokes his thumb over my skin. It's a small bit of contact, but it helps.

"No. Mom's fine. And so am I, thanks for asking." *But Joey isn't. Joey never will be again.*

"What is it, then? I'm...busy."

Yeah, with your fuck du jour, *apparently.* "I need to talk to you. I'm coming to see you. Today."

$\mathcal{M}$ILES

WE PULL up in front of a rundown house on the outskirts of Billings. Back in the thirties it must've been prime real estate, but now? It backs up to the interstate, and the roof looks one windstorm away from being blown off.

There are more weeds than grass in the front yard. A rusty bucket sits in the cracked driveway. A dog barks from a neighbor's house as I walk around the truck to take Sadie's hand.

"You grew up here?" I ask, trying to think of her as a child in this environment.

She shakes her head and sighs. "No. I lived with my

mom." Her gaze eats up the same grim scene as me. "It looked better when I saw him last."

Sadie didn't say much on the drive, other than giving me directions. I didn't push because the answers she's looking for seem to lie with her father alone. We can talk and talk but we won't get anywhere.

I open the rickety screen door and Sadie bangs on the door. No doorbells in a place like this.

It's opened a few seconds later by an older man who bears a passing resemblance to Sadie. Same hair color—although his is mixed with gray. Same eyes, but bloodshot and tired looking. Other than that, Curt Hopkins looks nothing like his daughter.

He scoffs. "I don't know why the fuck you came."

What's with his attitude? The prick.

She holds up a hand so I stay quiet.

"Joey's dead," she says.

He doesn't reply—in fact, he doesn't look all that surprised—just steps back and lets us inside.

The stench of stale cigarette smoke is overpowering. A white porcelain ashtray next to a threadbare couch is overflowing with butts, and the walls are tinged with yellow from the smoke. A haze of it blurs the air.

A platinum blond woman with sun-damaged skin dressed in a stained T-shirt and tiny shorts comes in from what appears to be the kitchen. She skates her gaze over Sadie and focuses on me. She actually licks her lips.

Man, in her dreams. I feel like I need a tetanus shot just looking at her.

Sadie's dad drops onto the couch, which squeaks beneath his heavy load. He clearly hasn't exercised in years—his beer belly tells the tale. Is he trying to kill himself with bad habits?

"Rainey," Curt tells the woman, "get me a beer."

Sadie tenses beside me but doesn't say anything to her father about the beer at ten in the morning.

"How'd you hear about Joey?" Curt finally asks.

"Coroner called me."

Interesting. The coroner didn't call Sadie. We heard it from Peterson. But perhaps Sadie doesn't want to tell her father she's a cop.

Curt doesn't offer us a place to sit, and Sadie doesn't move from inside the doorway. We're not staying long. Good. I feel like I need to take a bath in penicillin already.

Rainey returns and hands Curt a can of Schlitz. She grabs a cigarette packet from under her butt, pulls out a smoke, and lights it.

Sadie clears her throat. "Do you know why Joey might've been on Bridger land?"

Curt perks up and wipes his mouth with his forearm

after he takes a swig from his beer can. "Bridger? You mean that rich fucker?"

Sadie nods.

"Last I saw Joey, he was working for a freight company. Said he got a new assignment. A big one." Curt flicks his gaze to me. "Who the hell are you?"

"Bodyguard," I say. No way in hell am I telling him who I am. Or what I am to his daughter.

Curt grunts. "How'd he die?"

Sadie shrugs. "We don't know yet."

"Then why the hell are you here? If you don't have money or something, we've got nothing to talk about."

I set my hand on Sadie's shoulder to remind her she's not alone. I don't want her in this fucker's company a second longer than she needs to be, family or not.

"Did he leave any stuff here?" she asks.

I never thought of that. This place is tiny. An old miner's shack or something. No way her dad and brother both fit in this place, especially if Rainey lives here too.

"In the garage. He left a pile behind. Not sure the condition it's in."

Sadie eyes her father, who's lighting a cigarette of his own. "I'll go see what he left."

"Take it, otherwise it'll go to the dump."

Rainey climbs in Curt's lap, her gaze never straying

from me. She sticks out her tits—clearly outlined since she's not wearing a bra—and winks at me.

Using my hold on Sadie's shoulder, I turn her around and steer her outside. I ensure the door is shut behind us.

We both take deep breaths. We'll have to wash our clothes to get the scent of smoke out.

"Back there." She points around the back of the house.

I follow her down a dirt driveway to a building with a serious lean at the back corner of the property. I envision a vintage car stored in there, but I doubt anything but junk's filled the space in years.

The door is a side-slide, rollers above that make the wood move to the left. Sadie tugs on the handle, but I move her out of the way.

"Careful. Watch out for rusty nails and splinters." It finally gives and opens wide. Not sure if it'll close again, but that's not my problem.

Old tires, a lawn mower, and roughed-up boxes fill the space. A hole in the roof in the back corner has water stains down the wood walls. The floor is dirt, and the only light is from the sunshine.

Sadie enters, lifts box lids, tosses them aside. She pulls out an old football. Some clothes. I help her rummage for a few minutes. These things are clearly her brother's.

She lifts a stack of papers, sets them on top of an unsearched box. I move to stand beside her.

"Employment paperwork for Racehorse Hauling. A handbook."

I take it from her when she moves on. Based out of Billings. Nothing exciting.

"Here's a notebook. This is Joey's handwriting." She moves outside to get better light, flipping through the pages.

"It talks about barrels and chemicals. I'm not a chemist so I don't know what it means. Addresses."

I look over her shoulder. "The zip code for all those addresses is where Bridger Ranch is."

She runs her finger down the list. "Those aren't addresses. They're… I don't know. Code or something."

I look at her. "It connects your brother to the ranch."

"There's a phone number scrawled in the corner."

I pull out my cell, type in the numbers she reads off.

"Gene Chubb," the voice says.

"I'm calling for Joseph Hopkins."

There's silence on the other end.

Sadie's looking up at me.

"And you are?"

"A friend," I reply.

"I think you have the wrong number. No one here by that name."

"Right." I hang up and stare at the highway fifty feet away.

"What was that about?" Sadie asks.

"If it was a wrong number, why ask me who I am first?"

"What are you thinking?"

I'm not exactly sure, but I have more pieces of this fucked up puzzle than Sadie does. "I have a hunch. Not a good one, but there are a lot of coincidences. I mean, what are the chances of me falling for you and then your brother ends up dead on my land?"

She frowns. "What are you saying, that I tracked you down?"

I shake my head. "I think that was fate or destiny or something." It seems weird saying that, but it was the best answer I have. "But I think you ended up in Bayfield for a reason."

She blinks. "I don't understand."

"I don't either. Yet."

I call Chance and set the phone to speaker mode.

"Where the fuck are you? That tractor's not getting fixed without you," he grumbles.

"I'll fix anything that's broken. Later. Listen, I'm with Sadie. Get Shankle on the horn and tell him to call the DOJ person who's in charge of the case against Bridger Investments. Tell him it looks like Joey—Sadie's brother— was working for some company called Racehorse Hauling."

"Okay," he says slowly. "What are you thinking?"

"I think he was undercover for the EPA."

Sadie gasps, her eyes wide. "That he was working for a trucking company because—"

"Because he was trying to find dirt on Jonathan," I explain.

"And he was killed because someone found out," Chance adds. "It's possible. But why does the DOJ want to freeze our assets now? Jonathan's dead. So's Sadie's brother." He pauses. "Sorry, Sadie. I'm not trying to be insensitive."

"It's okay. Overwhelming, but it makes sense. I didn't know about the investigation. Peterson definitely doesn't."

"Have Shankle call the person on the case," I say. "I have a feeling it might be a guy named Chubb. Maybe they're doing this to see if something about their missing agent comes up."

"Or a dead body," Chance replies grimly.

I look to Sadie, cup the back of her head. "Right. Maybe there isn't any actual case, only them trying to find a missing one of their own."

Chance sighs. "I like your thinking. I'll call him right now."

"We're on our way back. Hopefully you'll have news for us by the time we get there."

I hang up and lean down to meet Sadie's eyes. "You okay?"

She nods. "Yeah. Joey being with the EPA is good. Doesn't make him any less dead, but I always wanted him to be a good guy."

"I'm not sure if my thinking is on track or not, but it's the only thing that makes sense. Too many flying parts for them not to be connected somehow."

"I don't want to share this with Peterson until...or *if* it pans out."

"Only one way to find out." I look at the house. "You want to say goodbye?"

She shudders. "Nope. It seems we both have shitty dads."

20

SADIE

MILES and I don't talk a lot on our way back to Bayfield, which is just as well. My mind is tumbling with facts and analyses, only everything is disjointed into words and phrases. I'm a good cop, a good detective. My thoughts aren't usually this jumbled.

We grabbed any kind of papers and notebooks that were in boxes, leaving behind everything else, which I doubt is headed to the dump. That'd take too much effort for my father. I don't want to miss a bit of evidence that might help find Joey's killer.

When Miles pulls up in front of my place, I turn to him. "I don't want to go in there."

"Okay. Where do you want to go?"

"Can we go back to your place? I don't want to be alone."

"Of course, baby. But you know I have to talk to my brothers about what we learned today."

"I know. I can deal."

"No problem. I just thought you might want to be alone."

I let out a sarcastic chuckle. "Alone is the last thing I want to be right now. Even though I hadn't seen my brother in so long, I thought I'd made my peace with all of it. Apparently I haven't."

"Of course you haven't. He was your brother." Miles kicks the car back into gear.

"This is my case. Well, *was*, if Peterson didn't pull me. But we've got some real leads in Joey's stuff. I'm in this thing no matter what."

He nods. "We'll go back to my place. I need to talk to Chance and Austin, maybe even get in touch with our attorney."

"Didn't you ask Chance to do that?"

"Yeah, I did, but I don't know if Shankle—that's his name, Tom Shankle—will even talk to us on a Sunday." Then he shakes his head with a low chuckle. "Although for what I'm sure we pay him, he'll probably come out and give us a foot massage on a Sunday. If not, I know a guy in New York I can call."

I smile, sort of. Miles does so much for me, and if he can get me to smile he's sure doing something right.

We stay silent again as we drive back out to the ranch.

A car—a really nice car, a Lincoln maybe? I don't know shit about cars—sits in the long driveway heading to the Bridger house.

"What did I tell you?" Miles says. "That's Shankle's car. I guess we can both get a foot massage today."

This time a smile doesn't come because I know, if an attorney is in the house, we're going to be talking about Joey. About his body. Not just about the visit with my father today.

Maybe it wasn't the best idea to come here.

"Hey," Miles says, clearly sensing my discomfort, "I can show you where my room is, and you can lie down. Or you can sit out on the back deck. There's a hot tub out there. It has soothed my muscles and joints many a night after Chance worked my ass off around here."

"I don't have a suit with me."

His gaze heats, but then he says, "Carly's here. She can probably find you something."

"I'm a lot bigger than Carly."

"Then you can wear one of my T-shirts. Or you can go naked." He winks. "No one's going to care."

I shake my head. "As much as a dip in the hot tub sounds like heaven, if you guys are going to be talking about Joey, I need to be involved. Besides, I'm a professional detective. I'll probably have some insight. Please don't try to keep me away because you think I might get upset."

I keep myself from laughing at my own words. All during the ride home all I could think of were pieces and chunks of information that I couldn't make sense of. I likely won't be any help at all, but I should be there. No matter how much I don't want to.

"Whatever you want, baby." Miles gets out of his truck, comes around to the passenger side, and opens the door for me.

He's such a gentleman. He's such...

He's just everything. Miles Bridger is simply *everything*.

How did he come to mean so much to me in such a short time? Am I being overly needy?

Whatever it is, I don't have the energy to question it right now.

Miles takes my hand, and he leads me to the front door, where we enter.

Sure enough, Chance and Austin Bridger—along with

Carly—are seated in the large living room along with a man wearing a white button-down shirt, jeans, cowboy boots, and a black bolo tie.

The attorney, I presume.

Chance and Austin both rise. The attorney rises and turns, his gaze falling on me.

"Who's this?" he asks.

"This is Sadie Hopkins." Miles slips his arm around my shoulder. "She's the sister of the deceased and a detective on this case. Sadie, our lawyer, Tom Shankle."

Mr. Shankle walks toward me, his hand outstretched. I take it and force myself to give a good firm shake. I learned long ago that, because I work in a field dominated by men, I need to give a strong handshake.

Louisa, the housekeeper, bustles in from the kitchen, her hair wrapped up in a tidy bun. "Ms. Hopkins, good to see you again. Can I get you two anything to drink?"

Only then do I notice the tall glasses of fresh lemonade sitting on the coffee table in front of each person.

"I could sure use a beer right about now," Miles says, "but I'm thinking it's better to keep my wits about me."

Austin gives him a smile. "I think we could all use a drink, but this lemonade's pretty good."

"You got a shot of Jack to put in that?" Miles asks Louisa.

She begins to respond but Miles gestures her to stop.

"I'm kidding, of course. Maybe after dinner, though." He turns to me. "You want some of that lemonade?"

I nod. I'm not a huge lemonade fan—it's a little sweet for me—but if I try to talk, I may choke or stammer.

"I'll get you each a glass right away."

"Thanks, Louisa," Miles says.

I open my mouth to mumble a thank you, but only a squeak ekes out.

Yeah, I need to keep quiet until I've got a handle on myself.

Miles tightens his arm around me, holds me close. "Come on. Let's have a seat."

Mr. Shankle and Chance are sitting in the two armchairs, a lamp table between them. To the right, Carly and Austin sit on the sofa. That leaves the loveseat for Miles and me, across from Mr. Shankle and Chance.

Loveseat.

And it hits me. Just with that word.

Loveseat. *Love.*

I've fallen in love with Miles Bridger.

It's not because I'm in a needy place right now, though I am.

And it's not because he's the most talented lover I've ever had, though he is.

It's because there was something between us—something more than the pure physical chemistry we share—from that very first night at Jody's.

I felt it then, and all it's done is grow.

I love this man. I flick my gaze to him. Big. Brawny. Protective.

But honestly? I can't give him what he needs right now. If he even wants a relationship. He's been pretty clear about his past, although he also said it's different with me.

Hell, look at what his family is going through. Look at what *my* family is going through. My father may be a dickhead of the first degree, but he just lost his only son. I lost a brother. My mother lost her firstborn child.

God, my mother. I've got to talk to my mother.

Miles takes my hand and entwines his fingers through mine. He's making it clear that we're together, and I like the feeling. I need to belong to someone right now. It helps.

Carly's eyes snag on our joined hands and smiles.

"I've been telling your brothers," Mr. Shankle says, "that I can check on the names involved with the EPA investigation first thing tomorrow morning. These are government workers, so no one's answering the phone today."

"Wait," Miles says. "I just called the number that I gave you guys when we were at Sadie's dad's place. Someone named Gene Chubb answered."

Mr. Shankle clears his throat. "He's not answering any longer."

"Damn. That call must've freaked him out." Miles turns to Louisa, who has returned with our lemonade. He takes one glass and hands the other to me. "Thank you, Louisa."

This time I will my voice to work. "Yes, thank you." I take a sip, and yes, it's sweet, but it's also comforting in a strange way.

My mom used to make lemonade just like this when I was young. It was Joey's favorite. She didn't make it after the divorce though. It was either unsweetened iced tea or water. Maybe that's why I don't like lemonade. It reminds me of Joey. Of what I lost after our family fell apart.

"We think your call probably raised red flags for this guy," Chance says.

"Why?"

"Well, that's what we need to find out." Mr. Shankle pulls his phone from his front pocket and glances at it. "I've cleared the next couple of days to work on this."

"We appreciate that," Austin says.

"Will you be coming with us to the meeting in the morning with Detective Peterson?" Miles asks Mr. Shankle. "The coroner's cleared Austin and me by time of death alone, but that leaves Chance. It might be best if he has legal representation at this point, especially if Joey really was EPA. Killing a government official is even more of a big deal."

He nods. "Definitely."

"Detective Peterson said Austin and I don't need to be at the meeting," Miles says. "Just Chance and Sadie. But fuck that. I want to be there." He turns and meets my gaze. "I'm not letting you go through this alone."

He squeezes my hand, and I smile.

Sort of.

Then he glances at Chance. "You either."

"Ditto that." From Austin, who squeezes Carly's thigh.

"So what are we looking at here?" Chance asks. "There can't be too—" He stops abruptly and looks at me.

I chew on my lower lip. "We all know who the body is. We know it's my brother. We can't keep tiptoeing around it."

"I agree," Carly says. "You can think you're doing the right thing by not talking about stuff, but it's never the right thing. I should know."

A haunted look passes over her face, but Austin tips her chin toward him and he kisses her. She smiles and it's gone.

"You're right, Carly." Chance gazes at me. "I'm sorry, Sadie. Your brother's body—"

"Joey. Joseph Hopkins." I look down at my lap. "That was his name. I think it's important that we say his name."

"Good point." Chance nods. "Joey. We all know that it's Joey." He sighs. "Honestly, I never knew him. But either he was here on our property, or someone wants us to think he was."

"Yes," Mr. Shankle says. "The body could've been planted after he was killed."

"That's where our department comes in," I offer. "We'll do an investigation. I'm sure the coroner can tell by how he died, drowning or not."

"Have you thought about recusing yourself from this case?" Mr. Shankle asks. "You are related to the deceased and clearly close to the Bridgers."

My cheeks warm, and I choke back a sob.

"Shankle, come on." Miles squeezes my hand again.

"She just told us she doesn't want us tiptoeing around this," the attorney says.

"You're right." I gulp back the sob. "I suppose I could recuse myself, and Miles pretty much told the lead detective I should be off the case because of all the conflict of interest. But it's *my* brother and well, Peterson is an asshole. We're the only two detectives here in this county and he's going to need all the help he can get in solving this, no matter what he thinks."

Mr. Shankle raises his eyebrows. "Only two detectives in the county?"

"It's a rural county, Shankle." Chance rubs his forehead. "How could you be our father's attorney all these years and not know that?"

He purses his lips as if the lemonade is way too tart. "I've told you before. I was his personal attorney. I handled ranch business. I never interacted with law enforcement."

"Maybe you should have." Austin frowns. "Seems he was into some shady shit."

"None of which came to light until his death," Mr. Shankle replies.

"And you had no idea?" This from Austin again.

"I wasn't paid to have ideas," the attorney says. "I did my job."

I clear my throat. I actually have something to add. "We've never needed more than two detectives before. We've got a sheriff, we've got several deputies, and we've got Peterson and myself. It's not like Bayfield is crime central."

Miles turns to me. "Maybe Shankle's right, baby. Maybe you should step back. You're too close to this."

He's right, of course, but for some reason I'm feeling argumentative. "Do you want Peterson—and only Peterson?—taking care of this?"

"Fuck no. Well, she's got me there, Shankle," Miles says. "Mark Peterson may be a good detective. I don't know, because I haven't lived here that long and all I've seen of him is when he's being an ass. But he clearly hates us. He had beef with our father. Hell, who hasn't?"

"Your father did have his faults." Mr. Shankle clears his throat, this time sounding a lot like Rainey did this morning. The man's clearly a chain smoker.

"You think?" Austin shakes his head.

"I was his attorney for twenty years," Shankle replies. "The man had a good side too."

This time Chance scoffs, raking his fingers through his auburn hair. "I lived with him my entire life. If he had a good side, I'd love to know about it."

"He gave a lot to charity."

"Right." Austin lets out a sarcastic huff. "It took a lot out of him to write all those fat checks. Maybe he should have floated a little cash to my mother over the years. To Miles's mom, too."

"I don't have any information on his relationships with any of your mothers," Shankle says. "But he didn't *have* to support charities the way he did. He gave millions of dollars to childrens' hospitals."

"You think he did it because he was altruistic?" Chance holds up his empty glass and stares at the ice in the bottom. "He did it for tax deductions. Or for virtue signaling. Whatever the reason, it wasn't for charity."

Silence reigns, and I guess it's up to me to break it.

"So there's no way to know, until tomorrow, whether Joey was working with EPA?" I ask.

"Nope. I can either be on the horn trying to find out that information, or I can be with you all in Peterson's office."

"Get one of your associates to look into Gene Chubb and the EPA," Austin says. "You do have associates, don't you?"

"Of course, I do. But your father didn't like for me to use them. I'm the only one he trusted."

I stop myself from raising an eyebrow. Jonathan Bridger trusted this guy and no one else? Big red flag. One I'll make sure Miles doesn't overlook.

"We are not our father," Chance says. "We are your clients now. I want this looked into first thing in the morning."

"You got it." Mr. Shyster—er...Shankle—makes a note in his phone.

I take another sip of the sweet lemonade. It soothes my throat, which still aches from the sobs I gulped down.

Louisa enters from the kitchen. "Lunch is ready. I set a place for Mr. Shankle and Ms. Hopkins."

The lawyer stands. "Thank you, Louisa, but I can't stay. I'll see you first thing in the morning, nine a.m. in town at the station."

Chance stands and sees Mr. Shankle to the door.

"You're staying for lunch." Miles says to me, not asking. Commanding.

"I'm not sure I can eat," I admit.

He reaches out, strokes my hair. "You have to keep your strength. This'll drive you crazy if you don't."

"It's already doing that, Miles."

He leans over and kisses my lips. "You're not alone. Do you hear me, Sadie? You're not fucking alone."

21

$\mathcal{M}$ ILES

I WATCH over Sadie like a hawk and make sure she eats at least one taco. I down five myself. This whole thing–our father, Joey's body, the mystery surrounding all of it–is such a clusterfuck, and I'm feeling every morsel of pain that Sadie is, but I never lose my appetite. Once lunch is over, I'm tempted to take her to my room and help her forget everything, but instead, I want to focus on her. On her needs. Not mine.

Perhaps they coincide. But if they don't? Her needs are going to come first.

These feelings I'm having for her are...disturbing. So unlike me. I'm totally focused on a person besides myself.

I've never been a selfish lover—any woman who goes to bed with Miles Bridger is always satisfied—but after that, I rarely think of the woman again. What she may need, what she may want. They knew the score going in. But this, with Sadie? Neither of us were keeping score.

"Would you like to go on a walk?" I ask her. Getting her to forget with orgasms is an option, but I have to offer up others.

She shrugs. "I don't think I can. There's something I need to do."

"What's that? I will make it happen."

She sets her small hand on my bicep. "You can't make this happen. Only I can."

I give her my best grin. I can definitely give her orgasms if that's it. "Try me."

She gives me a light swat. "I need to talk to my mom. I need to tell her about Joey."

Shit. Right. Of course she does. I think so little of my own mother that I forget other people have one. One who understands love.

"Why did you go to your father first?" I ask. It's not like they got along.

"You know why. Because I thought he might have information on Joey and what he was doing. Even if this Chubb guy turns out to be a dead end, I'm still glad I went. It's always good to be reminded what an asshole the man is."

"Baby..."

"You don't forget stuff like that," she continues, "but you romanticize certain things over the years. For example, I haven't seen much of my father since I was eight, so I tend to focus on the good memories I have other than the bad. Or should I say, the one or two good memories as opposed to the dozens of bad ones."

That's where Sadie and I differ. I never met my father and I don't have one romanticized memory about my mother. At all.

"Do you want to tell me about one of the good ones?" I ask, prodding her to open up, at least about the upbeat things.

Shaking her head, she steps back. "No. I don't want to give my father any thought right now. I need to figure out how I'm going to tell my mom that her son is dead."

He's been missing for a few years. Sadie hasn't heard from him and she didn't mention that her mom had. "She probably already suspects it."

"Well, of course, she does. We both did. But this is final, you know?"

I stroke her hair. That makes sense. "I'm not trying to

belittle this. Forgive me when I don't say the right thing. I don't have a lot of experience with…"

Her head tips to the side as she looks up at me. Right now she looks so much smaller. Tiny. Fragile. "With what?"

"Well, with death, other than my father, who I didn't even know. But I was thinking more along the lines of caring about another human being. My father didn't give a shit. My mom was more interested in her latest man than me. I don't really know what it's like to be cared about. Or to care about someone in return. The way I care for you."

Her cheeks flush a sweet pink. "Thank you. I care for you, too."

"I'm glad to hear that. This is all so fucking new. And we're coming together at a shitty time, but I sure wouldn't change meeting you. Not for anything."

She draws in a breath, attempts a smile. "Will you come with me again? To Billings, to see my mother?"

I'm tempted to ask her why we didn't see her mother this morning when we were already in Billings, but I don't. She had her reasons. Or maybe she didn't think of it. Or maybe she did, but she needed a break. Whatever it is, I'm not going to throw it in her face.

"Of course. Don't you want to call first?"

She shakes her head. "I really don't. I'll have to tell her

why I'm coming or make some excuse. I don't want to lie and I can't tell her this over the phone. I just can't."

"I understand. What if she isn't home?"

"She'll be home. She's a hairdresser, and she works six days a week. Sunday is the one day she closes her shop."

"What if she's out running errands?"

"If she has errands, she closes the shop for an hour or two or she does it in the evening after work. She's pretty adamant about keeping her Sundays free."

I nod. "Sounds like a woman who knows her priorities."

"She's not perfect," Sadie says. "But she did her best and she doesn't deserve the news I'm about to give her."

"When do you want to leave?"

"Now?"

"Absolutely. For you? Anything."

———

AN HOUR LATER, we're in a trailer park outside Billings.

"Is this where you grew up?" I ask.

"No. My mom sold the house I grew up in after I graduated from high school. She used the proceeds to buy her own beauty shop, and then the excess to buy the place here. She keeps it up real nice. I think you'll like it."

"I'm sure I will." I might be inheriting a billion, but I

came from humble beginnings. Started my own shop just like her mother.

She directs me to a well-kept mobile home on the property, freshly painted a light sage green. The windows have darker green shutters, and a few lawn chairs sit outside the door on the small lot. A Ford Fiesta sits in the parking spot next to the home. Non-pretentious living at its finest. Sadie's right. I like it.

I get out of the truck and walk to the passenger side to open the door for Sadie. I give her my hand and help her out and then she stares at the small home.

She walks the few steps to the cement stoop and knocks. I follow her.

A dog yaps behind the door, and when it opens, a woman who could be Sadie's older twin—same dark hair, only it's cut in a short style, and the same facial structure and slightly prominent chin—answers.

"Hey, Ma," Sadie says.

"Shoo!" Sadie's mother says to the small puppy.

He slinks into another room.

"What are you doing here, honey?"

"Do I need an excuse to see my mom?"

"Of course not. Come on in." Then she eyes me. "And who's this?"

"This is Miles. Miles Bridger." Sadie reaches toward

me and I take her hand. "Miles, this is my mom, Brenda Hopkins."

"It's a pleasure, Ms. Hopkins." I hold out my other hand.

She takes it and smiles. "It's Brenda. Everyone calls me Brenda. I could never pull off Mrs. or Ms."

"Brenda it is then."

The little dog—looks like he's a cross between a schnauzer and a Yorkie—struts back out.

"And who's this?" I kneel and give the dog a pet on the head.

"That's Princess. And she is a princess for sure. Now that you've given her love, she won't leave you alone."

"That's okay. I love animals. Good thing, since I find myself living on a ranch."

"Oh, you're a rancher?" Brenda asks.

"Sort of."

"It's a long story, Ma." Sadie leads me into the small living area inside the trailer. "We need to sit down."

"Of course. Please do. I'm afraid I was planning to go to the market tomorrow after work. I don't have anything to offer you other than water."

"That would be great." I smile.

"Coming right up." She scurries the few steps into her kitchen.

"You okay?" I ask Sadie.

"Yeah. Not like I have much of a choice."

"There's always a choice, baby," I tell her, "but you're strong. You can do this. And I'm right here with you."

Brenda returns with two glasses of water and hands us each one. She takes a seat in a chair opposite the loveseat where Sadie and I are sitting. Those two pieces encompass all the furniture in the small living area.

Brenda wipes her hand over her forehead. "To what do I owe the pleasure of seeing you both today?"

Sadie clears his throat. "It's about Joey."

Brenda gasps, clasps her hand to her heart, her eyes wide. "Oh my God. Has he been found?"

There's no mistaking the hope in her pretty brown eyes. Sadie looks down at her lap, clearly upset that she didn't choose her words better.

"Not exactly," Sadie says. "Not the way you mean."

Brenda frowns. "What are you trying to say, Sadie?"

Sadie turns to me, her eyes glistening. But she won't cry. Already I know she won't. She'll be strong for her mother. For herself.

"Miles, could you..."

"You sure?"

Sadie nods.

"The two of you are freaking me out here." Brenda flickers her gaze between us.

I take a sip of my water to soothe my parched throat.

"Brenda, I'm so sorry to let you know, but your son's body has been found."

Brenda gasps again, her hand flying to her mouth.

"I'm so sorry, Ms. Hop— I mean Brenda."

Sadie rises then, brings her mother to her feet, and embraces her.

Brenda cries, and Sadie rubs her back.

I'm not exactly sure what to do, so I pet Princess, who somehow ended up in my lap.

They take a few minutes, and then they break their embrace.

"I suppose it's good to finally know," Brenda says.

Sadie nods. "None of this is good, Ma. But you're right. At least we don't have to wonder anymore."

"How do you know all of this? Where was he found?"

Sadie nods to me again.

"He was found on the Bridger ranch," I say, speaking carefully. "His body was found by a creek."

"What was he doing—"

"Before you jump to conclusions," Sadie says, "Miles and his brothers didn't have anything to do with any of it. If anyone on the Bridger land was involved, it was their father, Jonathan Bridger, and he—"

"He's dead." Brenda looks my way. "I read about it. I'm sorry for your loss."

"Don't be," I say. "I didn't even know him. He's dead

and buried. And he left my two half-brothers and me with a big mess. But we're dealing."

Brenda fidgets with a strand of her hair. "I need some time to process this."

"Of course you do," I say.

"Does your father know?" Brenda asks Sadie.

Sadie sighs. "Yeah. We saw him this morning. He was his usual affable self."

"Oh God, baby doll. I'm sorry you had to deal with him."

"It's okay. He's harmless, really. He did give us what Joey left in the garage. It was mostly stuff to donate, but I was able to find a few things and possibly some information. We don't think he was really working for a trucking company."

Confusion creases her brow. "Then what was he doing?"

"We're not sure," I say. "Our working theory is that he was doing undercover work with the EPA."

"The Environmental Protection Agency?" Brenda sniffles. "Why?"

"I don't know, Ma. Maybe he got interested in the environment. You and I really didn't have a lot of contact with him after the divorce."

"That was Curt. Curt poisoned him against us."

"I'd like to think Joey had enough intelligence not to

listen to our father." Sadie sighs. "There's something else we need to think about, Ma. We should have some kind of memorial for Joey. Once we're able to take possession of his remains."

Brenda nods. "I suppose you're right. I never wanted to have one when I thought he might still be out there."

"You were holding out hope," Sadie says. "And I know I wasn't all that supportive about that. I'm sorry. I'm glad you had hope."

"I did. But now it's gone, Sadie. Joey's gone."

"Joey's gone," Sadie echoes. "But we still have each other."

22

SADIE

I DRIVE with Miles to the station the next morning for the meeting with Peterson. Not that I even have my car. Chance and Austin take Chance's truck, and Mr. Shankle is supposed to meet us there.

I still haven't talked to Miles about the attorney I met yesterday. After spending the rest of the visit with Ma making some preliminary arrangements for Joey's memorial, I didn't have it in me to talk about anything else.

I stayed at Miles's house last night, not wanting to be alone. Heck, I didn't want to be in bed alone. Not when I know what it's like to have Miles beside me. Have him hold me. He pulled me into his arms and spent hours making me forget about Joey, my father, everything. Even my name.

Miles and I are the last ones to arrive at the station, which doesn't look good on me, being that I work there. I'm sure everyone by now has heard about my brother's death.

We walk through the station, and the receptionist waves to me and offers condolences and then tells me that Mark is in the small conference room waiting.

We enter, and Mark, Mr. Shankle, Chance, and Austin are all seated around a small round table.

Peterson nods to the coffee maker in the corner. "You know what to do, Hopkins."

I don't particularly want a cup of coffee—and Peterson's a chauvinistic dickhead—but it will keep my sweaty hands busy. I glance up at Miles. "Coffee?"

He doesn't look happy and glares at the back of Mark's head. "Sure. Thank you."

I grab two Styrofoam cups—when the hell are we going to stop using non-recyclable Styrofoam?—and fill them. "Cream and sugar?" I ask Miles.

He shakes his head.

The station's coffee is sludge, but caffeine is caffeine.

"Now that everyone's here," Mr. Shankle says, "let's talk about clearing my clients' names."

"I've already cleared Austin and Miles," Peterson replies.

"I understand that. Mr. Chance Bridger is equally innocent in all of this. I want to get his name cleared, and then we will cooperate to the fullest extent of the law with the investigation on the Bridger property."

"Excuse me, Your Honor, but—"

"Your Honor is reserved for judges. I'm an attorney, Mr. Peterson."

I resist an eye roll. Peterson knows this. He's just being a jackass.

"Very well, Mr. Shankle," Peterson continues, "you will cooperate to the fullest extent of the law no matter what, whether I clear Mr. Chance Bridger or not. And do you want to know why?"

"I suppose you're going to enlighten me." The lawyer adjusts his bolo tie, clearly withholding laughter.

"You will cooperate because it is the law. We have every reason to believe a crime was committed on your client's property since the body was found there. We'll be searching more than just around the creek."

"Since I'm a lawyer and I'm here representing my client, I assume you have the necessary warrants to execute your investigation?"

Peterson shoves some papers across the table. "Authorized by a county judge first thing this morning."

Before Shankle looks at the documents, his phone buzzes on the table beside him and he glances down. "Excuse me, but this is my associate in Billings. He's looking into some things for me, and I have to take it."

"Absolutely," Chance tells him.

Mr. Shankle rises, exits the conference room, and closes the door behind him.

"Mark," I say, settling into a chair beside Miles, "what's it going to take for you to clear Chance?"

"A little investigation."

"Everyone in this room, including you, Peterson," Miles says, "knows that Chance didn't have anything to do with Joey Hopkins's death."

"I know nothing of the sort," he counters.

"You want to know what I think?" Miles asks.

"Not particularly," Peterson says dryly.

"I thought you wanted us to talk, to give you information? If that's the case, shut the fuck up and just listen. I think you're pissed off that you can't get me for this, so you're going after my brother."

"You? You think I'm after *you*? I already cleared you. You accusing me of being a dirty cop, Bridger?"

Miles shrugs. "I'm just stating an opinion, Peterson. You've had it out for me since you found me at Sadie's place."

"You'd be well advised not to say another word, Bridger." Peterson adjusts his necktie.

I give Miles a soft kick under the table.

Chance is a little less subtle.

"Shut the fuck up, Miles," Chance snaps. "Shankle's out of the room. If he were in here, he'd tell you to button it."

Miles opens his mouth, so I give him another kick, this one harder.

Peterson is essentially harmless, but he *will* bend the law when he has to, and if he wants to make Miles Bridger's life miserable? Or Chance Bridger's, as a way to get to Miles? He'll do it. He won't manufacture evidence, but he'll do everything up to that point, and he'll make them jump through so many damned hoops before he clears Chance that they won't be able to see straight.

Peterson opens his mouth to speak—

But the door opens, and Mr. Shankle walks back in.

At the academy, we took a course in body language and facial expression. We learned how certain emotions present themselves on a person's face and in their mannerisms.

Shankle must be a damned good attorney, because I sure can't read him right now.

"Ready to continue?" Peterson asks.

"Oh, yes." Mr. Shankle takes his seat. "I think you will be interested in what I have to say."

"And what's that?"

"Before we speak further, I'm going to have to ask you to leave the conference room, Mr. Peterson. I'd like to speak to my clients in private."

Peterson stands, which surprises me. I expected him to fight that. Instead—

"Very well. Hopkins, you're with me."

Now I see what he's after. He doesn't want me involved in whatever Shankle has to say to the Bridger's.

"Why the hell does she have to leave?" Miles says.

"Because she's a detective on this case."

"You need to recuse yourself, baby," Miles says to me. "You and I both know that."

It's not what I want to do, but it really is necessary in this case, not just because of my involvement with Miles Bridger but because the victim is my brother. I have major conflicts of interest.

"If you recuse yourself," Peterson says, "I can't guarantee you're going to have a job."

Miles stands then. "You've got to be kidding me." He stalks toward Peterson, his hand raised, finger pointed in his face. "She's the sister of a victim and she has a clear conflict of interest. There's no basis for losing a job. Right, Shankle?"

"Miles," Mr. Shankle says. "As your attorney, I advise you to stop right there."

"You'd best listen to your attorney there, Bridger." Peterson is visibly sweating at his hairline.

He should be. Miles Bridger is an imposing presence.

Mr. Shankle continues, "Like my client said, I hope you know you just threatened this woman's job based on her recusal when she has a clear conflict of interest in this case. I'm not sure what your sheriff would have to say about that."

Peterson says nothing. He just slinks out the door without asking me to leave with him again.

Miles takes his seat and grabs my hand. "What have you got?"

"I'm glad you're here, Ms. Hopkins," Mr. Shankle says, "because this definitely concerns you as well as the Bridgers."

It's amazing that my life is intertwining with Miles's, but I never expected it to go down like this.

$\mathcal{M}$ILES

WE SIT in silence as Shankle recounts what he found out from his associate.

"Apparently you were on the right track," Shankle says, looking at me. "Joseph Hopkins was involved with the EPA. But not in the way you might think."

Sadie's eyes widen. "So he wasn't a trucker? He wasn't hauling freight?"

"Not exactly. You may or may not know, Ms. Hopkins, that the Department of Justice is getting ready to open an investigation into some properties owned by the Bridgers."

She drops her jaw. Obviously, she didn't know.

"We had nothing to do with any of this, Sadie." I set my hand on top of hers.

Chance shakes his head. "Hell no."

She blinks. "Right. I know that, of course. But...I thought you all were ranchers."

"You don't make billions solely by raising beef," Shankle says.

"Our father had outside investments." Chance shifts in his seat. His big frame makes the chair squeak. "Several of which were apparently violating EPA regs."

"What kind of investments?" Sadie wonders.

"You'd be surprised at what kind of companies have hazardous chemicals to dispose of," Shankle says. "Hospitals, for one. Any business that uses paint, and that's a lot. Any type of industrial cleaning company. Heck, any kind of industrial business. Mining. Oil. You name it. Jonathan Bridger dabbled in all of those and more. According to the DOJ, he cut corners with hazardous-waste disposal."

"Why would Jonathan Bridger cut corners like that?"

I squeeze Sadie's forearm. "From what I've gathered, he was a shitty man. All he cared about was money, pure and simple. Proper disposal of hazardous chemicals costs a lot of money. Doing things right is a lot more expensive than doing them easily. I should know. I have to adhere to strict regulations when I'm disposing of motor oil and other chemicals I use in my business in New York."

"Does it really cost that much to follow regulations?" Sadie pushes.

"More than you think. For a small operation like mine, it's not going to break the bank. But for Bridger? He probably saved millions by not following the rules."

Sadie rubs her forehead and then her temples. "So we've already determined that your father wasn't a good man. But how does Joey fit into all of this?"

"He must've been working undercover for the EPA," Chance says. "Right Shankle? Or maybe the FBI or the DOJ?"

"First of all"—Shankle clears his throat loudly—"the DOJ doesn't operate undercover. But your brother wasn't working for the government, undercover or otherwise."

Sadie blinks at him and then leans back in her chair. Damn! I really thought my angle was right, and I convinced her of it too.

"What exactly was he doing then?" I take a sip of my coffee, which is now cold. I grimace at how bitter and awful it is. "What the hell is this?"

"I should've warned you." Sadie stares down at the table. "The coffee here is shit."

I raise my eyebrow at her. Shit? It tastes like the industrial waste my father dumped illegally.

"It's not that bad." Austin pushes his cup away from him. "Compared to diesel fuel, anyway."

"Are you going to answer my question?" I push. "What was Sadie's brother doing if he wasn't working for the EPA?"

Shankle clears his throat once more. I swear to God the man is about to lose a lung.

He leans forward, sets his forearms on the table and scans Chance, Austin, and me. "He was actually working for your father."

Sadie's cheeks go white. "Holy shit."

I squeeze her hand. "Baby, I'm sure there's a reasonable explanation."

"There must be," she says. "Joey was good. He would never do anything against the law."

I squeeze her hand again. She wants to believe the best of her big brother. But Sadie has said herself that she hadn't seen him in forever. Had little to no contact with him since she was eight years old. And I've seen what her old man is like. Joey could easily be the apple that didn't fall far from the tree.

God, I hope he wasn't. For Sadie's sake.

"Apparently your brother was working for a business called Racehorse Hauling," Shankle says, "a freight company based out of Helena."

That matches the paperwork we found in the old garage.

"A couple of your father's companies hired them to haul what turned out to be barrels of hazardous chemicals across the border into Canada."

"So he *was* hauling freight into Canada," Sadie murmurs.

"Why?" Chance asks. "Are the laws for hazardous chemical disposal less stringent in Canada?"

"I'm not an environmental lawyer," Shankle says. "But according to my associate who looked into this matter, the United States and Canada have an agreement regarding the transboundary movement of hazardous materials."

"Then why was our father transporting the stuff to Canada?" Austin asks.

"Because Canada has something the US doesn't," Shankle says. "Lots of vast vacant land. From what I understand, Ms. Hopkins, your brother didn't know he was transporting hazardous chemicals across international lines. But he was given explicit instructions about where to cross the border and which border agent to deal with."

I shake my head. "A border agent who had been paid off."

"Give the boy a—"

Austin's cheeks burn red. "If you say give the boy a

silver dollar, I'm going to fly across the table and pound on you, Shankle."

I can handle Shankle, but after what went down with Carly, Austin has zero patience for the guy. I have to admit, he is a patronizing fucker.

"So my brother's innocent." Sadie heaves a sigh of relief. "Although in the eyes of the law, he was the one committing the crime."

"That's true. As far as we know, he didn't know what he was hauling." Shankle makes some notes on his yellow legal pad.

"This doesn't explain how he ended up on our property," Chance says.

"There will still be an investigation," Shankle says. "Apparently Racehorse Hauling was shut down a few years back. Your father was never implicated in anything, until recently."

"The whistleblower who came forward after he died." Austin glares at Shankle.

"Give the boy a Benjamin." Shankle lets out a gravelly laugh. "There. I just gave you a ninety-nine dollar raise."

Austin seethes across the table.

"Did your associate find anything else out?" Chance asks, keeping Shankle moving so Austin doesn't kill him.

"Something that would get you off the hook for this?" Shankle shakes his head. "I'm sorry, son."

"I'm not your son," Chance says. "You did my father's dirty work all those years. How do we know you're not behind all of this?"

"You're well within your rights to request another lawyer." Shankle scoots his chair back and crosses his legs. "But I've told you before, I only took care of his ranching business, and I swear to you everything there is legit. Besides, if I'm aware of a crime, I have to report it."

"Doesn't mean you will," Austin mutters.

"Chance makes a good point, Shankle," I add. "There's got to be someone at your firm or another firm who might be a better fit for this particular case, especially since everything points to your dead client."

"We had this discussion already," Shankle counters. "I've got one of my partners who is experienced in white-collar crime work looking at this. As for me? All I can say is look at my track record. I took care of Jonathan Bridger for several decades. He had his faults for sure, but I never saw any evidence of malfeasance in my dealings with him."

"So you're sure he operated his ranch on the up and up?" Austin taps his fingers on the table.

If he didn't, it could impact our inheritance. I didn't want dirty money, especially any that might have been involved in killing my woman's brother.

"To the best of my knowledge. I knew he had outside

interests, but he never commingled any of the funds with this ranching business. Now, that doesn't mean that his estate is exempt from the fines and civil penalties with regard to the EPA violations."

"Don't they have to prove it first?" I say.

He nods. "Yes, but in a civil case, the burden of proof is much lower."

Chance runs a hand over his face. "We've got enough going on. We need you to make the EPA case go away. Surely there's more than enough to pay any fines and damages from my father's other holdings."

"We have to sell off assets," Shankle says. "Nothing is liquid."

"Then sell the damned assets," I say, my voice rising. "Do you really think any of us care if we own some hospital or paint supply company or hazardous chemical plant?"

Sadie tenses beside me.

"You okay, baby?"

She nods, and then she sniffles. "I just don't understand the whole thing about Joey. I mean, who's this Gene Chubb who answered the phone?"

"My associates haven't gotten that information yet," Shankle says. "The phone wasn't traceable. But they're working on it."

Sadie nods. "Okay."

"We'll prove that your brother was a good guy," I tell her.

She turns to me, meets my gaze, and then she looks across the table at Chance. "My brother's dead, Miles. It's more important that we prove to the world that *your* brother is a good guy. We need to get Chance off the hook for Joey's death."

My God.

This woman. I can't believe it, but I'm falling hard. Hell, I already fell hard.

"Anything else?" Austin asks our attorney.

"That's all I've got for now. I suppose we need to let Peterson back in."

Sadie rises then. "I'll go get him. I think... I think I'll go sit at my desk and try to get some work done. I'm off this case, but I do have others."

I trail my fingers over her forearm. "You could take a few days off. Don't you have bereavement pay or something?"

She nods, sniffling again.

"Then take it, baby. Take some time. Deal with your loss. I know it's not simple, but you're entitled to it."

"I'll think about it, Miles. I'll tell Peterson he can come back in."

Sadie leaves the room, and all I want to do is run after

her, hold her, promise her that no one will hurt her ever again.

But I need to stay here with my brothers. With our attorney. With the detective on this case.

Peterson comes back in, takes the seat he vacated earlier. "All right. What do you gentlemen have to say?"

Shankle coughs into a handkerchief and then clears his throat for the zillionth time before he rattles off the same story he just told us.

"Interesting." Peterson scribbles some notes.

"Are you ready to let Chance Bridger off the hook?" Shankle asks.

"Why would I do that?"

I stand, my hands curled into fists. Between my need to run after Sadie and make sure she's protected at all costs and this bizarre need to protect my newfound brother, I'm ready to fight. Fight like I had to when I was a schoolkid and my mother was married to Chris Ciancio, the Mafia dude from Hell's Kitchen. Husband number four.

"You're supposed to be a detective, damn it. How can you not see what's going on here? Joey Hopkins was hauling hazardous chemicals across the border, only he didn't know it. He probably went to the authorities, and Bridger had him taken care of."

I wince at my own words, but even though Sadie is

safe outside this conference room, I still don't like to think of her brother as being *taken care of*. Reminds me again of Ciancio.

"If that's the case, I'm sure it will come out of the investigation." Peterson doesn't meet my gaze.

"Look at me," I say. "Look me straight in the eye, Peterson."

He glances up, and I don't like what I see in his eyes.

"Watch your tone, Bridger."

"Fine. Do your fucking investigation. But when you're done, expect a lawsuit filed by the three of us for malicious prosecution, abuse of process, and anything else our team of highly paid attorneys can think of."

Yeah. My mom married an attorney along the way too, which blessed me with a little legalese.

With that, I whisk out of the conference room.

I'm not sure which one is Sadie's desk, or if she has an office, but I don't see her anywhere. I head to the reception desk. "Did Sadie Hopkins leave?"

The receptionist nods, batting her eyes. "She did. She said she was going to take a few days off."

"Thank you."

Good. Sadie took my advice. Now I just need to find her so I can take care of her.

I do feel a responsibility to my brother, but Chance can take care of himself. Plus, he has Austin and Shankle.

And Shankle will set him up with the best criminal attorneys in the state of Montana.

Right now? I need to see to my woman.

I laugh out loud at my own words.

My woman.

I've been thinking of her as my woman all this time.

Hell, I never even wanted a woman of my own. I was happy with many women and no commitment. I got all the pussy I wanted back in New York, and I never had to pay alimony. Lesson learned from every husband my mother dragged to divorce court.

Sadie drove with me this morning, so her car isn't here at the station. Her apartment isn't far, so she probably walked home. I get in my truck and drive the few blocks to her place.

I park on the street and a few seconds later I'm standing at her apartment door. I knock. "Sadie?"

No response.

There's no doorbell, so I knock again.

Then I fucking pound on the door. "Sadie? Where are you?"

Fuck, maybe she stayed in town, went to get a cup of coffee or something. Why wouldn't she tell me where she was going?

I drive back to the station, where Austin and Chance are now exiting, and get out of my car.

"What the hell was that about?" Austin demands. "The three of us have got to stick together."

"Yeah, you're right." I shift my gaze to the sidewalk. "I know I went off a little halfcocked."

"A little?" Chance lifts his eyebrows. "I don't like Peterson any more than you do, but it's my ass on the line, not yours. He's a good detective, but he's not above fucking with you if he's pissed."

"Yeah, I know. Sadie gave me the 4-1-1 on him."

"What the hell were you thinking, Miles?" Austin shakes his head at me.

"Hell, I was... Fuck. I was thinking that my woman just lost her brother. That she's sad. That she needs me."

They both raise their eyebrows at me.

I'm done hiding. "Yeah, you heard it. *My woman*. Sadie Hopkins is my woman. I'm fucking in love with her. Satisfied?"

Austin tries to hold back a grin but is ultimately unsuccessful. "Seriously? You're in love?"

"Don't you dare give me any shit. You fell faster and harder than I did."

"And you don't hear me complaining about it." Austin shuffles his feet on the sidewalk and holds out his hand to Chance. "Pay up."

Chance shakes his head, but he's smiling as he pulls

out his wallet and slaps a twenty-dollar bill in Austin's palm.

I roll my eyes and set my hands on my hips.

"The receptionist inside said Sadie was going to take some days off," I tell them.

"That was good advice you gave her," Chance says, tucking his wallet away. "Especially now that she's recused herself from our case."

"I just drove over to her place, but she's not there." I gaze around the sidewalk and street, absently looking for Sadie's brunette head.

"It's close to lunchtime. She might be over at Millie's. Or at that taco place." Chance rubs his belly. "I could stand eating."

"You're just like me." I chuckle. "The world might be caving in on us, but I can always eat."

"I'm the same way." Austin laughs. "My mom always said I'm a bottomless pit. That must be something we got from our father."

"I hope that's all we got from him," Chance says. "I don't want to be anything like that motherfucker. Thank God that none of us look much like him. We got his height and shoulder breadth. You sure favor your mother, Austin. Miles, I've never met your mother but I bet she's a blonde with blue eyes."

I nod. "That she is. Though she colors her hair now to hide the gray."

"My mom was a stunning redhead." Chance smiles.

I get the feeling there's a story there, but Chance doesn't elaborate.

Instead, he places his Stetson on his head. "So about that lunch? One of Millie's greasy burgers is calling my name."

I grab my phone. "Yeah, sure. Let me give Sadie a call first."

It rings.

And it rings.

Finally I get sent to voicemail.

This is Sadie. Sorry I can't get to my phone right now but let me know who you are and I'll call you right back.

Just the sound of her recorded voice brings a smile to my face.

"Hey, baby. It's Miles. Where'd you run off to? Austin, Chance, and I are headed over to Millie's for lunch. Meet us there, okay?"

Then I follow my brothers a couple buildings down to Millie's Diner. I know a burger won't solve our problems, but it sure can't hurt to try.

24

Sadie

Call it detective's intuition.

Or call it an old-fashioned hunch.

I walked back to my place after I left the conference room at the station, but I didn't go in. Instead, I got straight into my car and started driving.

I knew I had to go somewhere, though I wasn't sure where.

So it was as big a surprise to me as anyone when I ended up back at my father's place. I sit in my car staring across the street at the dilapidated house.

He's probably working, but if there's a way to get into

his house I'm going to find it. Breaking and entering isn't a good look on a cop, for sure, but I can always pull the "it's my dad's house" line. It's not even a lie.

Something has been itching at the back of my neck since yesterday. I feel like I missed something.

I pull into the rocky driveway and park my VW Beetle. Then I make my way to the ripped screen door, open it, and knock.

No response, not that I expected one. This neighborhood works during the day, or they keep to themselves.

I knock again, louder this time.

Again, nothing. So I turn the door by knob, and I'm surprised when it opens.

I didn't think my father would leave his home unlocked. I expected to have to find an unlocked window to crawl through. But it makes sense. There's nothing in here worth stealing.

I walk inside, and the stench of stale cigarette smoke and sour beer assaults me.

No problem. I'll breathe through my mouth. Time to have a look around.

"Who the hell is out there?"

I know that voice—that gravelly-sounding cigarette voice.

"Hello, Rainey," I call. "It's me. Sadie. Curt's daughter."

Rainey comes out from the kitchen, wearing a

magenta fluffy robe and holding a cigarette. "Don't you know how to knock?"

"I did knock. Several times. Very loudly."

"And then you decided to just come in?"

"Isn't a daughter welcome at her father's house?" I counter, although I'm pretty much only a daughter by blood, nothing more at this point.

"Curt didn't seem to welcome you yesterday. What are you doing here?" Her hair's up in a sloppy bun and mascara is smeared beneath her eyes.

"I want to see my father," I tell her.

"He's on a job. Somebody has to pay the bills around here." She flicks ashes on the light blue shag carpeting.

"Don't you work?"

"I'm between jobs, not that it's any of your business." She takes a long drag on the cigarette and exhales the smoke through her nostrils and her mouth.

"When will my father be home?"

"Dinner time."

At the mention of dinner, my stomach lets out a growl. It's lunchtime—an hour past, actually.

"Have you eaten?" I ask.

"Do I look like I've eaten?"

I'm not sure what that's supposed to mean. Her diet probably consists of potato chips and cigarettes.

A light goes off in my brain. They say the way to a

man's heart is through his stomach. Maybe the way to my father's girlfriend is to get some food into her deprived body. "Would you like to go to lunch, Rainey?"

She drops her arm to her side and flicks more ashes on the worn carpet. "Do I look like an idiot to you?"

She really doesn't want me to answer that question.

"I'm hungry," I say. "It's lunchtime. I'm going to get something to eat. Would you like to come along?"

"Who's paying?" She eyes me suspiciously.

"Who do you think is paying? I invited *you*, Rainey, so of course it's my treat."

Her eyes narrow. "What's your game, sister?"

If she's shacking up with my dad, I'm definitely not her sister.

"I don't think there's any game involved in inviting someone to lunch."

She pauses a moment, moves her gaze over and around me. "Yeah, yeah. I could eat. Let me get some clothes on." She heads down a tiny hallway and disappears behind a door.

I take advantage of the few minutes to scout out the living room where Miles and I stood yesterday.

The worn sofa is the same dull brown color, and Rainey hasn't bothered emptying the overflowing ashtray sitting beside it on a veneer end table. A couple of empty beer cans litter the floor, and a copy of *People* sits on the coffee table, open to a story about the Kardashians.

The blinds are open, letting some sunshine in, and the walls are the same yellowish white.

I pick up the beer cans and walk into the small kitchen. It's actually in better shape than the living area, but not by much. Dirty Tupperware bowls are piled in the sink, and a loaf of store-bought white bread is sitting out, the plastic bag still open. I twist the bag closed so the bread won't get stale.

I pick up empty cans again. If I were a recycling container, where would I be?

Then I laugh out loud. If the Bayfield Sheriff's Office can't recycle, my father certainly—

But I lift my eyebrows when I spy both a green container—sporting the triangular recycling symbol—and a black container sitting by the back door.

I'll be damned. My father just went up a notch in my book. He recycles.

Of course, one notch doesn't get him very far.

I toss the beer cans in the green container, and then I head back into the living room to grab the ashtray. Why not tidy up a little? This guy did father me, after all. As preposterous as that may seem.

I head toward the ashtray, but I'm waylaid by Rainey, who appears from behind her closed door now wearing skinny jeans and Iron Maiden T-shirt. Her platinum hair is pulled back in a ponytail now and her raccoon eyes are gone. If it weren't for the scarlet lipstick, she actually wouldn't look too bad. The fine lines marring her skin cover what was once an oval face with high cheekbones and a nicely defined jawline. Unfortunately, the years of cigarettes and alcohol have taken their toll.

"What's your favorite place to eat around here?" I ask.

"Curt and I never eat out," she says. "So I'm not really sure. There are a few places up the road a bit. I can show you."

"Sure. We can take my car."

"Good thing, seeing as I don't have one."

We walk out the door, and she clicks the key into the deadbolt, locking it. We get into my car, and she pulls a pack of cigarettes out of her purse.

"Sorry. No smoking in my car." No way in hell is my car going to smell like an ashtray.

She scoffs, but she puts the cigarettes away. "Just go on out to the right, up the street, and then turn right onto the main drag. There's some places a couple miles up."

I follow her instructions and then I clear my throat. "So...how long have you and my dad been together?"

"About a year and a half."

"So you didn't know Joey. My brother."

She shakes her head as she looks out the passenger

window. "No, he was long gone by the time Curt and I got together."

Her tone is nonchalant, and I try not to be bothered by it. If my father doesn't care about his own son, why should she?

I inhale a breath, determined to keep my cool.

"Did my dad ever mention him?"

"Nope."

"I suppose that's not surprising," I say, "seeing how he never mentioned to you that he had a daughter either."

She turns, and I feel her gaze on me as I watch the road through the windshield.

"You know, you look kind of like him. Like Curt."

"Actually I look a lot more like my mom."

"She must be a pretty thing. You sure are."

I stop my eyebrows from flying off my head. Did my father's girlfriend just give me a compliment?

"Thank you."

She sighs. "I wish I were young and pretty again. Those days are long gone. Enjoy your youth, honey. It's gone before you know it."

"How old are you, Rainey?"

"Not a day over thirty-five." She cackles out a laugh. "I'm actually forty-three. Just had a birthday two weeks ago."

"Happy belated birthday. This can be your birthday lunch, then."

"Sadie, honey, I've got your number. You don't have any interest in having lunch with me. You're here to get information about your father."

"That's where you're wrong," I tell her. "I'm here to get information about my brother."

She laughs. "I don't know anything about him."

"I didn't say I was here to get information from *you*, Rainey. That's an interesting name, by the way."

"It's short for Lorraine. Lorraine Lucille Thompson. I'm not even kidding. Did you ever hear such an awful name?"

I chuckle. "I think it's kind of pretty. It's better than Sadie."

"You don't like your name, either?"

I slow for a stop sign and put my blinker on to turn right. "I've never liked it. I always wanted one of those pretty names like Ashley or Brittany or Jordan."

"Isn't your dad's mother named Sadie?"

It's surprising my father shared that piece of info with her.

"Yeah. The original Sadie Hopkins. But I hate the name, because people used to make fun of me in school. They called me Sadie Hawkins. Said no guys would ever ask me out. You know, because the Sadie Hawkins dance is when the girls ask the boys out?"

"Stupid kids." Rainey fiddles with her purse.

"Yeah, stupid kids. But I got through it." A couple of restaurants come into view on the left side. "Are these the places you were talking about?"

"Yeah, pull onto the side road there, and you can take a look. I think there's a Mexican place, a Japanese bowl place, and a sandwich shop. What do you feel like?"

"It's your birthday lunch. What would *you* like?"

"I'd really like a nice fat steak, but none of these places are going to have that."

"How about a roast beef sandwich?" I gesture to the sandwich shop.

"That sounds fine."

I pull into a parking spot on the street. Then I exit the car, and Rainey and I walk toward the sandwich shop called Nora's Delights. I look around the area, because I've got the strange feeling that I've entered an alternate dimension. I'm about to have lunch with my father's girl-friend, who I just met yesterday, and who I have nothing in common with. Still, this could help my investigation somehow. Rainey doesn't know anything about Joey, but maybe I can get some information about my father.

I may have recused myself and gone on bereavement leave, but I'm not letting this go.

We walk into the restaurant and a server waves at us. "Sit wherever you'd like, ladies."

"Over there looks good." I point to a table in the corner.

"Works for me."

Rainey and I take a seat at the table. She grabs one of the menus from the holder and opens it.

"So how's my father's business going? The construction."

"Same old, same old. He loses more bids than he gets these days because of his drinking."

I'm surprised she admits that to me. "Oh? He was doing well when he and my mom got divorced. Of course that was twenty years ago."

"Did Curt drink when you were a kid?" she asks.

The waitress stops by with glasses of water.

"Not that I remember." I grab a glass and take a sip. "At least not to excess. But I was only eight when they split up so I'm sure there was stuff I didn't notice."

"He can't stay away from the beer. He's lost a lot because of it."

"How about you?" I ask. "Do you drink beer?"

"I like a cold one every now and then, but I can go without." She gestures to the *No Smoking* sign on the wall. "That's my vice. Smokes. I've tried to quit, but I just can't."

"Have you tried those patches? Or that gum?"

She rolls her eyes at me as if I'm an idiot. "Honey, that's just nicotine in another form. None of that helps."

"How about hypnosis?"

"You mean like seeing a therapist or something? How the hell would I pay for that?"

She's got me there. "You said you're between jobs. What do you do?"

"Whatever I can get. I was working up at the paper mill out on the edge of town, but I got laid off a couple months ago. I look around every now and then, but there isn't a lot of stuff out there for a high-class career girl like myself." She lets out a garbled chuckle.

I'm not sure what to say, so I silently thank the universe when our server returns.

"What can I get you ladies today? You want to start something to drink besides water?"

"Iced tea," I say. "Unsweetened."

"Got it. And for you, ma'am?" The server—Amy, her tag says—nods to Rainey.

"Iced tea sounds good to me too. And I'm ready to order. I'll have the steak sandwich, hold the sautéed onions, with a large side of fries."

I scan the menu quickly. "I'll have your roast turkey and avocado on a croissant."

Amy makes a few notes. "I'll get these right up for you ladies and I'll be back in a minute with your drinks."

I set my menu back in the holder.

Rainey pulls out her phone, swipes at the screen a few times. Smokers' wrinkles line her lips, and her red lipstick is bleeding into them. I'm seeing her in a new light. She's not a bad person. She's just had some bad luck. She's a nicotine addict and she's hanging out with my father. Not a good combo.

"My dad still owns the construction business, doesn't he?"

Rainey looks up from her phone. "Yeah. But like I said, he doesn't get the bids he used to. Or that he claims he used to get. I've never seen him do great. He's off work more than he's on these days. He says he used to have the best reputation in Billings, but now he's kind of known as a drunk. He has to underbid to get any work at all, and you see how we live."

That does suck. "I'm sorry. I mean, he and I aren't close, as you saw. But he's still my father."

"I love the big lug," she says. "Sometimes I don't know why, but I do."

"Love doesn't always make sense."

My words ring true. I've known Miles Bridger for mere days, and I'm so in love with him my heart hurts. I miss him right now. Actually *miss* him. What makes sense about any of that?

"I had a great guy once," Rainey says, a smile easing

onto her lips. "We were young and in love, but I made a lot of mistakes."

"We all do that."

"I suppose. I just didn't know what I had back then. He wanted to get married and go off to college together, but I was young with a tight body and a pretty face, and the thought of four more years of school sounded like a prison sentence. I didn't want to give up my nightlife. So he went off to college and married someone else, and I partied hard and had what I thought was the time of my life. And now look at me. The best I can do is a minimum-wage job, and as soon as there's a downturn in the economy, I get laid off. I should've been out there learning a skill instead of drinking and experimenting with drugs. I should have married Jeremy and gone to school." She lets out a sad laugh. "That's sure a downer. I'm done talking about me. What do you do?"

"I'm a detective."

Her eyebrows rise. "Private detective? Or cop?"

"I'm a cop."

Her eyes are wide. "No shit?"

"Yeah. Didn't my father tell you?"

"Honey, he didn't even tell me you existed."

"What about my brother? Did you know *he* existed?"

"I knew about Joey. They had some falling out is what

he said, and then of course you know he disappeared those years back."

I gulp. "Falling out?"

"Yeah. Curt didn't have a lot of good to say about his son. He was always angry that he didn't go into the construction business with him, and he blamed him for losing all his money."

"I thought he was going to work for my dad after the divorce." I frown. "And what money?"

"You didn't know? A couple years ago, Curt came into some money."

I widen my eyes in total surprise because it didn't look like the man had a dime to his name based on the house. "He did?"

"Oh yeah, I know you can't tell from the way we live." She read my mind. "But apparently it was somewhere in the mid six figures."

"Did he have any of this money left by the time you met him?"

"Not really. From what I hear he went to Las Vegas and blew a big chunk of it, and the rest of it trickled away because he got less and less work and drank more and more beer."

I wrinkle my forehead. This isn't making any sense. "How did he come into this money? I'm not following."

The waitress returns with our drinks and Rainey

reaches for a sugar packet in the holder in the center of the table. "I didn't know him then, but it was some kind of investment. That's what he says, anyway." Then she darts her gaze around the restaurant as two women come in to eat. "I'm not sure I should say anymore."

"Why not?" I take a sip of the iced tea Amy delivered. Yuck. It's not fresh brewed.

"Curt won't like that I'm talking to you about this." She grabs a spoon from the napkin roll in front of her and stirs her drink. She's suddenly nervous.

"I'm his daughter. I have a right to know what he's doing."

"I'm afraid he doesn't see it that way. I should've kept my big mouth shut."

Amy returns with our sandwiches, and Laney stops talking altogether.

She doesn't say another word as she stuffs her face with her steak sandwich and fries, and when she's reduced them to a few crumbs, she gestures to Amy and orders another sandwich with onion rings to go. Rainey's not thin, but I have a feeling she hasn't had this good of a meal in a while. I happily pay the bill for her extra food.

She chatters about mundane stuff on our drive back, and then she gets out of the car when I pull into the driveway. "Thanks again, Sadie. I enjoyed the lunch."

I'm not ready to give up my search yet. "You mind if I use your bathroom?"

"Sure, that's fine. Come on in."

She opens the rickety screen door, unlocks the front door, and I follow her inside.

"Down the hall, first door on the left." She points, but I doubt I need directions in a place this small.

I walk over the carpet to the bathroom. It looks about how I expected. Nothing more than a bathtub, a shower curtain decorated with palm trees and coconuts, a toilet, and a sink. The hand soap dispenser is empty. Great.

I don't actually have to go to the bathroom, but I take a look around. In the mirrored cabinet above the sink is a man's razor and a bottle of aspirin. No drugs. Not that I expected to find any. Rainey's drug of choice is clearly nicotine, and my father's is alcohol.

Still, I'm relieved. My father may be an asshole, but at least he's not a drug addict.

I flush the toilet for show, and then I turn on the faucet, try to extract whatever's left in the soap dispenser, and then wipe my hands on my jeans. I don't want to touch the hand towel.

Rainey's in the kitchen, smoking a cigarette.

That reminds me of the ashtray in the living room that I wanted to empty. I walk into the living room and pick it up. A cigarette butt falls onto the end table. I grab the cigarette butt, place it back in the ashtray—

Crash!

The ashtray slips from my still damp hands and clatters onto the glass-topped coffee table, shattering it. Butts and ashes fall to the table and to the floor.

"You okay in there?" Rainey yells from the kitchen.

"Yeah. Fine. I'm sorry. I dropped your ashtray. It broke the glass top of the coffee table. I'll clean it up and replace the glass."

What a mess.

I pick up the ashtray, ready to shove as much ash back into it as possible, when the design printed on it catches my gaze.

It's a horse. A racehorse, to be exact, and next to it... I look on the other side, next to the horse logo.

Racehorse Hauling.

Perhaps this was Joey's. Maybe he gave this ashtray to our father.

But already, my instinct is telling me otherwise. If my father truly came into some money—if he was telling Rainey the truth—this could be a clue. And when Racehorse Hauling was shut down? So was the money.

I pull my phone out of my purse quickly, and my heart skips a beat when I see that I have a voicemail from Miles. I didn't hear the phone ring because I set it on silent during the meeting in the conference room this morning. Crap. I forgot to turn the ringer back on. I hope Miles isn't worried. I call his number, but he doesn't answer.

I'll send him a text.

Miles, I'm at my father's. You're not going to believe what I—

Damn. Instead of hitting the space key I hit *send*. Sheesh.

I continue the text, but then I jerk and drop my phone onto the floor among the ashes and butts.

The knob on the front door is turning.

Slowly.

I look up and swallow hard. Oh shit.

25

Miles

I PULL out my phone to try Sadie again and—

Damn! I've had my ringer off since this morning. And I have a missed call and a text from Sadie. Thank fuck! I'm not sure I realized how worried I was until the cement block rises from my shoulders.

Miles, I'm at my father's. You're not going to believe what I—

The text stops. And she didn't leave me a voicemail.

The cement block is back, and it's heavier than ever this time.

Why the hell is she back at her father's place? He clearly had no interest in her.

Why would she send an unfinished text?

From there?

My heart races. This can't be good news.

We've just arrived back at the ranch after lunch, and I'm getting ready to go check on the tractor Chance wanted me to look at.

The tractor will have to fucking wait.

My woman needs me. I feel it in my bones. No way would she leave me a half-assed text and nothing else.

Without bothering to tell my brothers, I race outside, scramble into my truck, and plug in the GPS coordinates from yesterday's visit to Curt Hopkins.

I make a quick call to 911 and then I gun it out of town.

26

Sadie

My father walks in, wearing jeans, a red and black flannel shirt, and holding a bright yellow hard hat. He looks me over, clearly not happy to see me. "What the hell are you doing back here?"

"Can't a daughter visit her father two days in a row?" I ask, sarcasm lacing my tone.

"I checked you out, Sadie Jane Hopkins," he says. "You're a fucking cop."

"I never hid that fact. You're my father. I assumed you knew."

"How the hell would I know?" he snaps. "You know I don't like cops."

"Uh...you're my *father*. Shouldn't a father know what his child does for a living?"

"Your mother never mentioned it."

I huff out a laugh. "When's the last time you talked to her?"

"Around the fifth of never." His gaze drops to my waist. "You armed?"

"I'm off-duty," I say.

It's not a lie. I *am* off-duty. But I'm also armed. My Glock is strapped to my ankle. Good thing boot-cut jeans came back into style.

Rainey ambles out from the kitchen, cigarette in her hand. "What are you doing home so soon?"

"Storm's coming in. We stopped for the day."

My father eyes the living room, the mess on the floor and the coffee table. "What the hell happened here?"

"I was going to empty the ashtray for Rainey, but I dropped it. I'll replace the glass."

"Damn right, you will." He nods to Rainey. "Get me a beer." Then back to me, "This mess isn't going to clean itself up."

All he sees me as is another woman to do his bidding.

"I'll take care of it." Rainey heads back into the kitchen.

"Did Joey give you that ashtray?" I ask.

He gives me a look as if I'm crazy. "How the hell should I know? It's just a damned ashtray."

"It's an ashtray with the logo for the freight company he was working for."

"So?" He drops his hard hat on the couch.

"Did you know the company is out of business now?"

"Why the hell would I know that? It's just a stupid ashtray."

"Rainey tells me you had some money a few years back," I add, pushing.

"Rainey is a damned liar."

I pause a moment. Listen for sounds of Rainey in the kitchen. There it is—the soft vacuum sound of the refrigerator door closing. She'll be back with his beer any moment. Did she hear him call her a liar? This place is tiny, so I'm betting she did.

"Is she?" I ask. "She said you got into some kind of investment, got six figures out of it, but blew most of it in Vegas. Probably blew the rest on beer and cigarettes."

"If you're looking for money, Sadie—"

I hold up my hand up to stop him. "I haven't taken a penny from you since I was eight years old, and I don't plan to start now. Besides, look at this place. You clearly don't have a pot to piss in."

"Then I suppose you can be on your way."

"I'll be happy to get the hell out of here," I say, "as soon as you tell me about Joey and Racehorse Hauling."

"Joey was a pain in my ass." My father runs a hand through his greasy hair. "I got him a sweet deal with that freight company."

My pulse quickens. "I think, Dad, that you're the one who got a sweet deal with that freight company."

He inhales with a snort, and for a moment I think he may hock a loogie right in his living room. "You don't know what the hell you're talking about."

I step forward and close the distance between us. "Don't I?"

"You've got a lot of nerve, coming here, snooping around—" he gasps. "Rainey, what the fuck?"

I turn, and then I nearly stumble over my own two feet.

Rainey stands, shaking, and in her hand is a Smith & Wesson nine millimeter pistol. An M&P with a polymer chassis, from what I can see. A gun widely used in law enforcement, but of course anyone can get one. They're costly, so how the hell does Rainey have one?

But the bigger question—and what's making my heart go a mile a minute—is that I've stepped close enough to my father that I can't tell whether she means to point it at him...or at me.

She cocks her head. "Sadie, I think you need to leave now."

My dad's a waste of space, but I don't want him dead. It's my job to protect people, and assholes are still people. "Rainey, what are you doing? I just bought you lunch."

"Yes, and I thank you. I've got nothing against you, but there are things you don't understand."

"I understand my brother's dead. And I think he's dead because he uncovered something about the company he was working for. When you told me my father came into some money, it got me thinking. Then when I saw the ashtray, with the Racehorse Hauling logo…"

"Just leave." Rainey shakes.

Damn. A gun in the hand of a frightened woman who's shaking is never a good thing.

"Look," I say, holding my hands up in front of me, "I can help you. I can help you get out of this dump."

My ankle holster burns against my skin. I don't perceive that Rainey is a real threat, but still I'm itching to get to my piece.

My father takes a step forward.

I suck in a breath. Rainey now has the gun trained solely on him, but before I can get my Glock, he's covering her hand with his own, easing the pistol out of her grip. "You give me that gun, sweetheart."

She nods, handing the gun over to my father.

I don't know whether this is good or bad.

But I find out quickly.

He turns and points the pistol at me. "Come on with me. Now."

I gulp, trying to swallow the dread that's speeding through my bones. "I don't think so."

"Sadie, you may be my flesh and blood, but when push comes to shove, I'm going to save my own ass."

I gulp again, this time audibly. So I'm right. Dad has a connection to Racehorse Hauling, and I'm betting it's not a good one. Now I know why my intuition was telling me to come back here.

But I didn't factor my own father holding me at gunpoint into the equation. Fathers aren't supposed to hold their daughters at gunpoint. In what world does this make sense?

My heart is racing so fast I'm afraid it's going to beat right out of my chest.

My father's gaze is cold—hard and cold.

While I'm trained to deal with situations like this, my own mortality flashes in my mind.

So much to do.

I want marriage. Children. I want a damned dog!

Mostly I want Miles.

I want all of those things with Miles Bridger. Miles Bridger, the man I love.

But I won't have any of it if my father pulls that trigger.

No. Won't happen. No father could kill his own child.

Except...

The blood in my veins turns to ice.

Maybe my father already *did* kill his child.

Maybe *he's* responsible for Joey's death.

And if so?

I can kiss my dreams—my *life*—goodbye.

27

MILES

Thank fuck.

Sadie's car is in her father's driveway.

Surely there's an explanation for the text—the unfinished one—she sent.

A patrol car is parked in front of the house from the frantic 911 call I made on the road. Two officers are seated inside.

I exit my vehicle and walk to the patrol car. "I'm Miles Bridger, the guy who called. Did you find anything, Officer?"

The blue in the driver's seat shakes his head. "The

only one home is a woman named Lorraine Thompson. She says nothing's out of the ordinary."

"My girlfriend was here earlier. This is her father's place."

"Yes, Ms. Thompson said your girlfriend was here and took her to lunch earlier. But she left."

I point to the driveway. "But that's her car. Her VW Beetle."

"Right. Ms. Thompson said Ms. Hopkins's car wouldn't start, so she called an Uber to take her home and said she'd arrange for the car to be towed later."

I rake my fingers through my hair. "And you believe all this crap?"

"Not really, sir, but we can't go into the house without probable cause."

"I can." I stalk toward the door.

"Sir? You can be arrested for trespassing."

"Do I look like I care? My woman's inside that house somewhere. And I'm going to find her. By the way, the woman I'm looking for is one of your own. A cop."

I stomp through the front door, not even attempting to knock. "Rainey? Where the fuck are you?"

Rainey emerges from the kitchen in a cloud of smoke, a cigarette dangling between her fingers. "Hey there, stud."

I stop a few feet away from her, setting my hands on my hips. "Don't give me that shit. Where's Sadie?"

"I already explained everything to the cops."

"Yeah, and it's all a bald-faced lie. Where is she?"

"How many times do I have to tell you? She's not—"

I jerk when a gunshot rings out. Holy fuck.

My heart plummets to my stomach. God, no. Not my Sadie.

I grab Rainey by her shoulders. "It sounds like it came from a basement or something. Underneath here. Where the fuck are they?"

Rainey chokes out a sob in her gravelly voice and points to a door right off the kitchen. "Basement."

I don't think. I only react. I race down the creaking wooden stairs to the basement, nearly losing my footing several times, but nothing will keep me from Sadie.

"Sadie? Baby! I'm coming!"

I reach the concrete floor of the basement, let my eyes adjust to the darkness.

Oh, God...

Blood seeps toward me on the ground.

No. God, please, no! Not Sadie, not my Sadie. I take a step, and—

In a flash, Sadie's in my arms, her small body hitting mine.

In my arms—warm, safe, sobbing.

My Sadie.

I kiss her wet cheeks. Her lips. The top of her head. I hold her so tight that she pulls away from me finally, gasping.

"My God, baby." I kiss her tear-stained cheeks. "What happened here?"

Then in the corner, I see. Curt Hopkins lies unconscious on the gray concrete floor.

"Is he—"

She shakes her head. "No. No. He's just unconscious. But he does need an ambulance. I shot him in the leg, and when he fell he hit his head on the floor."

"Fuck, baby. I thought—" I gulp in a breath. Then another. "I thought I had lost you. I thought I had lost the woman I love."

Her eyes widen, and she sniffs back another sob. "What?"

"I love you, Sadie Hopkins. I never thought love was possible for me, but I fucking love you." I pull her hard against my body. "Don't you ever scare me like this again."

She melts into me, her body sinking into mine, and murmurs something into my shoulder.

I hope she's telling me she loves me too, but in this moment? It doesn't even matter. All that matters is that she's safe. Safe in my arms.

The uniformed police officers stomp down the steps, their guns drawn.

"What's going on down here?" one of them asks. "Is everything okay?"

"I'd say everything's not okay." The other blue points to Curt bleeding and unconscious in the corner.

Sadie pulls away from me then, her face swollen and tear stained. "He's my father. He was holding a gun on me. I shot him in self-defense."

An officer raises his weapon and points it at Sadie. "Put down the gun!" he shouts.

"For fuck's sake!" I shield Sadie with my body, snag it from her hand, and five it to the officer. "Here."

"I told you what was going on, that I couldn't find her. Obviously the woman upstairs is a big fucking liar." I point at Sadie. "She's a cop, for God's sake."

The blue lowers his weapon. "This true?"

"Yeah. Detective Sadie Hopkins out of Bayfield. My badge is in my purse. It's probably still up in the living room. The injured party is my father, Curt Hopkins. He brought me down here at gunpoint."

"And the gun that shot him?"

"His own." She lifts the flared part of her jeans. "This is mine."

"You were able to overpower your father?" the first officer asks.

"Yeah. I've got the same training you guys have. It wasn't easy, but I managed. Plus, he's drunk."

"He's alive." The second officer goes over and holds his hand to Curt's neck. "The bleeding doesn't look life threatening yet, but he needs an ambulance."

"Already called," another blue says, walking down the stairway. They must have called in shots fired or something, getting backup. "I've got the other lady in custody."

Good. That woman needed to go to fucking jail. Jesus, she stood in the kitchen smoking a fucking cigarette while Sadie was down here defending herself from her gun-toting father.

"You work with Bryant?" the officer asks Sadie. "He's a good man."

Sadie nods. "He is."

"Detective, I'm sorry you had to go through all of this. Jones here will stay on the scene until the ambulance comes for your father. I'm going to need you to come down to the station and answer some questions."

I pull Sadie back into my body. "Whatever you need. But my woman isn't going anywhere without me. Ever again."

$\mathcal{S}$ADIE

"HE WAS STUMBLING A LITTLE, OBVIOUSLY DRUNK," I say, as the intake officer, Luis Reyes, makes his report. "I'm trained to read people, as you know, so I took a chance. As soon as I saw him waver, I clutched his wrist quickly, twisted it, and forced the gun out of his hand. He lunged at me, but I was able to grab the gun off the floor. He continued advancing toward me, so I had no choice but to shoot him."

"You're a good shot, Detective," Officer Reyes says. "You knew just where to hit him so you wouldn't do any lasting damage."

"It was tempting," I say, "but he is my father. And I don't want a dead body on my conscience, for sure."

Reyes nods. "A lot of us cops have been there. It's not pretty. But you did good, Detective. Sheriff Bryant is lucky to have you."

"Thank you."

I'm aware of how robotic my voice sounds. I'm still reeling from the events of the afternoon. I'm just stating facts, giving the details I know he'll want for his report. The emotions and feelings pushed to the side. Miles sits beside me, holding my hand.

Miles, the man I love. The man who loves me back.

"What's going to happen to my father?" I ask. "I mean, after he gets out of the hospital."

"He'll be arrested for assault with a deadly weapon of course, unless you don't want to press charges."

I don't reply at first. He *is* my father. But he's somehow involved in what's going on with Joey and the Bridger family, and it needs to be investigated. We need to prove Chance's innocence, and I personally want to prove Joey's, if I can. It'll all be a lot easier if Curt Hopkins is out of the way. Or at least talking.

"I will be pressing charges, Officer. I want to know why he did it. I was pushing him for answers he didn't want to give. Hopefully jail time will get him to spill."

"Good," Reyes says. "I didn't want to have to talk you

into it. I don't like to see a fellow officer dealing with the same shit we go on calls for day in and day out and then not press charges."

I nod in understanding.

"What will happen to Rainey?" I ask.

"Rainey?"

"Ms. Thompson," I clarify. "My father's...companion."

"She had a lot of warrants out for her arrest. Several unpaid traffic violations and one failure to respond to a jury summons. That's just to start. She'll be held pending arraignment unless someone comes to bail her out."

I sigh. Rainey. Is she one of the good guys or one of the bad guys? I'm not sure whether she knows herself. I chose not to mention that she held the gun on my father and me first and that she let him lead me to the basement at gunpoint. She's got enough problems. All I can do now is wish her well.

Miles squeezes my hand. "You okay?"

I glance his way, take in his concerned pale eyes. "Not in the slightest, but I will be." I sigh again. "I had lunch with Rainey today. She almost had me convinced she was a good person. I'm a detective. I should have known better."

"Part of her probably *is* a good person." Miles cups my cheek. "I think maybe you wanted to see something good in her. Or more accurately, you wanted to see something good in your father *through* her. You didn't do anything wrong, Sadie. You were just being a daughter."

I shrug and glance down. "I'm glad you think so."

"I know so. You're a great detective."

"I agree with Mr. Bridger." Reyes offers me a smile when I look his way. "Some of the most seasoned law officers couldn't have gotten out of the situation you were in today. Especially with a relative involved."

I nod. "That means a lot to me. Thank you."

"Is there anything else you need, Officer?" Miles asks. "Because if there isn't, I'd like to get this lady home."

"I think that's good for now. I'll need you both to be available for questioning as necessary."

"Absolutely. Whatever you need." Miles pulls me to my feet. "Let's get out of here, baby."

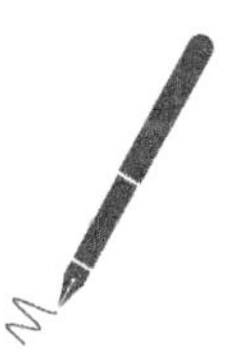

$\mathcal{M}$ ILES

HOLY SHIT. I think I aged ten years in the past two hours. Sadie can take care of herself. I've only known her a few days and she's done a good job so far, but shit... Dealing with a deranged, gun-wielding father and then shooting him to save herself?

Yeah, ten years.

I'm glad the fucker's going to jail. And staying there. Same goes for his crazy bitch girlfriend. I should be glad that we learned more about Joey's connection to my father because of our visit and garage hunting, but to have her almost killed? Not worth it.

Peterson can do his own fucking job.

We pull in front of the house and I shut off the engine. She's been quiet all this way and I haven't pushed her to talk. Processing everything and dealing with a fucked-up family is a lot. I'm here for her though. No chance in hell she's dealing with this alone.

Nothing's actually been resolved with Jonathan's past actions, her brother ending up dead on our land, the freezing of Bridger funds. Any of it. Jonathan's dead. So is Joey Hopkins. But Sadie's alive and I'm going to remind her of that.

"Come on, baby."

She looks my way and nods.

I go around the truck and open her door. Help her down. Keep my hands on her hips and her eyes lift to meet mine.

"When I want to clear my head, I go for a ride. That's how I first met you."

The corner of her mouth tips up.

"I was pissed about everything going on here and got on my bike. Found a random bar. Found a random woman who wanted to give me her panties."

"You still have them, you know," she says grumpily.

"Oh, I know. You're not getting them back either." I laugh. "But even if I hadn't gone on that ride, we'd have met anyway, you know."

She pauses, thinks it through. "Right, I was here the next morning."

"I'd have seen you then, wanted you just as much. We were fated."

"You, the big, brawny biker, think we're meant to be?"

"Abso-fucking-lutely." I close the space between us and kiss her.

She lifts her arms and circles them around my neck, tangling her fingers in my hair.

I lift her, and she wraps her legs around my waist. She's pressed against the side of the truck and my tongue tangles with hers.

"Get a room, you two," Austin calls from the front door.

Carly giggles beside him. Or I think it's Carly, because I don't turn. My focus is solely on Sadie.

I lift my head, look into Sadie's dark eyes, ignoring Austin.

"Should we go to my room?" I ask. "I've got lots of places I want to kiss you."

She smiles. "Yeah."

My dick, already hard, presses into her core.

I don't set her down, just turn and head up the steps. Sadie laughs, which is the best sound in the world.

"Sadie's father's an asshole. He wanted her dead in his grungy-ass basement. She shot him in the leg. He's in jail.

We learned more about her brother, but it'll hold until later."

Sadie's looking at me as I give Austin and Carly a quick rundown of what happened. Carly's wide-eyed and Austin's jaw is clenched tight enough to crack molars.

Sadie kisses my neck.

"Much later." I cut past the couple and into the house, down the hall, and to my bedroom.

I have no doubt Austin will update Chance. Shankle's doing his job and the intel we gathered on Joey's job can wait until I fuck my woman and ensure she knows she's mine.

I tell her just that when I kick my bedroom door shut with my foot.

"I don't know what's coming next, but I want to be with you when it happens."

"I thought you were going to kiss me," she says. "Everywhere."

I set her on her feet and start to peel her shirt over her head.

"Oh, that's the plan, baby. But I don't want you thinking I'm ignoring everything else."

"You are. We are." She pushes her jeans down her hips. "That's okay. I need you."

Her gaze lifts to mine. Meets, holds.

I growl, lean my shoulder down and toss her over it,

and then drop her on the bed. Her jeans were around her ankles and I pull them the rest of the way off. Her panties fly over my shoulder along with her bra.

She's bare before me.

"Fuck, you're gorgeous." I undo the button on my jeans and unzip them to give my dick some room. I don't dare take them off because it's all about Sadie right now.

Tugging an ankle, I pull her to the edge of the bed and drop to my knees. Kiss the inside of her ankle and then set it over my shoulder.

"I'll start here." I kiss up the inside of her leg. "Then here." I fan her core with my breath and then lick up her slit.

"Miles," she breathes.

"Everywhere. You're mine, Sadie. All mine."

And I do just that. Learning her body, backing up my words with tender actions. Then rough ones. Because my woman likes it every way I give her.

As long as we're together, everything will be just fine.

EPILOGUE

HANCE

Love.

I only loved one woman in my life, and that was nearly fifteen years ago.

Sure, I have my fun. I pick up a lady at The Dusty Rose now and again, maybe even take her out a time or two.

But that's it. I've only felt that spark once, and I've never found it since.

So I stopped thinking about love. Bachelorhood isn't so bad. I love the land, the animals, the work around the ranch. Hell, I even love my new brothers.

Damn it, though, the two of them brought romantic

love into the house. Within weeks. They had no trouble finding it right here in Bayfield, my hometown. To be fair, they didn't actually find love. Love seemed to find *them*. But love never found me, not in fifteen years.

Granted, I haven't exactly been looking, and life has been a fucking tornado since my father's death. I'm still a person of interest in the death of Joey Hopkins. I'm innocent, and I'm pretty sure the information Sadie uncovered will go a long way in proving it, but still...

It all gets to a guy after a while.

"I need to ride like the wind, boy," I say to Raphael, my midnight-black quarter horse, as I groom his flank with the curry comb.

I'm on my own at the ranch today. Miles is taking care of Sadie, who needs some serious time off. I haven't seen them and don't plan to. They haven't left his bedroom as far as I know, and I don't expect to see them anytime soon. Austin has gone with Carly to her therapy session in Billings.

So I'm taking the morning off too. Just Raphael and me and the sunshine.

I need an escape.

Ivory, a gorgeous cremello mare, snorts in the next stall. She's the horse Carly was grooming when Austin first laid eyes on her. He's told me the story a hundred times if he's told me once—how he was a goner the first time he saw her.

Miles says the same thing about Sadie. As soon as she sauntered up to him in that bar and asked him to take her panties, he was all in. Doesn't sound much like a love story, but the look in Miles's eyes when he tells it removes all doubt.

Maybe I should go over to that bar sometime.

"What do you think, buddy?" I brush a tangle out of Raphael's mane. "You think there's a woman out there for me?"

"I'd like to think there is."

That voice—melodic with just a touch of sexy rasp.

I drop the curry comb, and it lands on the hay-covered dirt with a thud.

I turn.

Standing in the door to the stable is a mirage.

A fifteen-year-old fucking mirage.

It can't be. It just can't.

"Avery? Avery Marsh?"

"Hello, Chance."

God damn.

She was just in my thoughts.

One woman. I've loved only one woman in my life. People called it puppy love, but I knew the truth. I knew what I felt was special.

My heart shattered when she left. She and her mother moved away a few months before our high school graduation, and I never heard from her again.

But here she stands.

I know the stable stinks of hay and horse manure, but I swear to God all I smell is the sweet citrus floral of Avery's perfume. She always smelled so good.

"I can't believe it's you," I say.

"I'm actually here on..." She looks down at her feet.

Her blond hair is pulled up into a loose bun, and she's wearing black pants, a white silky blouse, and a dark red blazer.

But I see her in cut-off shorts and a violet tank top, her silky wheat-colored waves tumbling over her shoulders.

That's what she was wearing the last time we saw each other.

Those were the clothes she put back on after we made love in that spring on the edge of the ranch. We took each other's virginity that day, and the next day she left.

"Here on what?" I ask.

"On business, Chance." She draws in a breath as she flips open a black case to reveal a badge. "I'm a special agent with the FBI."

"What? The EPA—"

"The EPA is doing its own investigation. I'm here about the death of Joseph Hopkins."

I shake my head. "I don't understand. We've been working with the local sheriff's office."

"Not anymore." She closes her badge holder. "As of now, the Feds are taking over this investigation. That means I'm here on Bridger Ranch until further notice."

Read the thrilling conclusion of The Billion Heirs! Read Chance's story now!

Chance Bridger may have been raised on the family ranch with the father who left him and his two half brothers billions, but he hated the man. Unlike his brothers, he can't escape his past, especially when it comes back to haunt him in the form of Avery Marsh.

BONUS CONTENT

Guess what? We've got some bonus content for you with Sadie and Miles. Yup, there's more!

Click here to read!

A NOTE FROM HELEN

Dear Reader,

Thank you for reading *Flawed*. If you want to find out about my current backlist and future releases, please visit my website, like my Facebook page, and join my mailing list. If you're a fan, please join my Facebook street team (Hardt & Soul) to help spread the word about my books. I regularly do awesome giveaways for my street team members.

If you enjoyed the story, please take the time to leave a review. I welcome all feedback.

I wish you all the best!

Helen

Sign up for my newsletter here:

http://www.helenhardt.com/signup

GET A FREE VANESSA VALE BOOK!

Join my mailing list to be the first to know of new releases, free books, special prices and other author giveaways.

http://freeromanceread.com

ALSO BY HELEN HARDT

Follow Me Series:

Follow Me Darkly

Follow Me Under

Follow Me Always

Darkly

Wolfes of Manhattan

Rebel

Recluse

Runaway

Rake

Reckoning

Billionaire Island (Wolfes continuation)

Escape

Gems of Wolfe Island (Wolfes continuation)

Moonstone

Raven

Garnet

Buck

Steel Brothers Saga:

Trilogy One—Talon and Jade

Craving

Obsession

Possession

Trilogy Two—Jonah and Melanie

Melt

Burn

Surrender

Trilogy Three—Ryan and Ruby

Shattered

Twisted

Unraveled

Trilogy Four—Bryce and Marjorie

Breathless

Ravenous

Insatiable

Trilogy Five—Brad and Daphne

Fate

Sex and the Season:

Lily and the Duke

Rose in Bloom

Lady Alexandra's Lover

Sophie's Voice

Temptation Saga:

Tempting Dusty

Teasing Annie

Taking Catie

Taming Angelina

Treasuring Amber

Trusting Sydney

Tantalizing Maria

Standalone Novels and Novellas

Reunited

Misadventures:

Misadventures of a Good Wife (with Meredith Wild)

Misadventures with a Rockstar

The Cougar Chronicles:

The Cowboy and the Cougar

Calendar Boy

Daughters of the Prairie:

The Outlaw's Angel

Lessons of the Heart

Song of the Raven

Collections:

Destination Desire

Her Two Lovers

Non-Fiction:

got style?

ALSO BY VANESSA VALE

For the most up-to-date listing of my books:

vanessavalebooks.com

The Billion Heirs

Scarred

Flawed

Broken

Alpha Mountain

Hero

Rebel

Warrior

Billionaire Ranch

North

South

East

West

Bachelor Auction

Teach Me The Ropes

Hand Me The Reins

Back In The Saddle

Wolf Ranch

Rough

Wild

Feral

Savage

Fierce

Ruthless

Two Marks

Untamed

Tempted

Desired

Enticed

More Than A Cowboy

Strong & Steady

Rough & Ready

Wild Mountain Men

Mountain Darkness

Mountain Delights

Mountain Desire

Mountain Danger

Grade-A Beefcakes

Sir Loin of Beef

T-Bone

Tri-Tip

Porterhouse

Skirt Steak

Small Town Romance

Montana Fire

Montana Ice

Montana Heat

Montana Wild

Montana Mine

Steele Ranch

Spurred

Wrangled

Tangled

Hitched

Lassoed

Bridgewater County

Ride Me Dirty

Claim Me Hard

Take Me Fast

Hold Me Close

Make Me Yours

Kiss Me Crazy

Mail Order Bride of Slate Springs

A Wanton Woman

A Wild Woman

A Wicked Woman

Bridgewater Ménage

Their Runaway Bride

Their Kidnapped Bride

Their Wayward Bride

Their Captivated Bride

Their Treasured Bride

Their Christmas Bride

Their Reluctant Bride

Their Stolen Bride

Their Brazen Bride

Their Rebellious Bride

Their Reckless Bride

Bridgewater Brides World

Lenox Ranch Cowboys

Cowboys & Kisses

Spurs & Satin

Reins & Ribbons

Brands & Bows

Lassos & Lace

Montana Men

The Lawman

The Cowboy

The Outlaw

Standalones

Relentless

All Mine & Mine To Take

Bride Pact

Rough Love

Twice As Delicious

Flirting With The Law

Mistletoe Marriage

Man Candy - A Coloring Book

ABOUT HELEN HARDT

#1 *New York Times*, #1 *USA Today*, and #1 *Wall Street Journal* bestselling author Helen Hardt's passion for the written word began with the books her mother read to her at bedtime. She wrote her first story at age six and hasn't stopped since. In addition to being an award-winning author of romantic fiction, she's a mother, an attorney, a black belt in Taekwondo, a grammar geek, an appreciator of fine red wine, and a lover of Ben and Jerry's ice cream. She writes from her home in Colorado, where she lives with her family. Helen loves to hear from readers.

Please sign up for her newsletter here:
http://www.helenhardt.com/signup
Visit her here:
http://www.helenhardt.com

ABOUT VANESSA VALE

A USA Today bestseller, Vanessa Vale writes tempting romance with unapologetic bad boys who don't just fall in love, they fall hard. Her books have sold over one million copies. She lives in the American West where she's always finding inspiration for her next story. While she's not as skilled at social media as her kids, she loves to interact with readers.

vanessavaleauthor.com

facebook.com/vanessavaleauthor

twitter.com/iamvanessavale

instagram.com/vanessa_vale_author

amazon.com/Vanessa-Vale/e/B00PGB3AXC

bookbub.com/profile/vanessa-vale

tiktok.com/@vanessavaleauthor

www.ingramcontent.com/pod-product-compliance
Lightning Source LLC
Chambersburg PA
CBHW072210150726
48002CB00005B/1752